Wendy Cooling

'I read it in one sitting! Really good
page turners are quite rare these days!'
*Hayley Warren, Librarian,
Amberfield School, Nacton, Ipswich*

'Girls are going to devour it! I can see
ven the lukewarm readers being hooked.'
*Jackie Spink, Head of English,
Deben High School, Felixstowe*

ORCHARD BOOKS
338 Euston Road, London NW1 3BH
Orchard Books Australia
Level 17/207 Kent St, Sydney, NSW 2000

ISBN 978 1 84616 342 5

3 5 7 9 10 8 6 4 2

Printed in Great Britain

deeper than Blue

JILL HUCKLESBY

ORCHARD BOOKS

For Chris and Maddy

I know this kid who can do perfect cartwheels, eat a whole tube of Pringles, get showered and dressed in four minutes flat, play 'Lord of the Dance' on the piano with her big toes, do a hundred sit-ups without getting cramp and pedal her bike backwards, perching on the handlebars.

She loves bands from the 1960s, (just like her dad), dancing on her bed singing into a hairbrush (just like her dad) and her favourite thing in the world is a triple scoop of dark-chocolate ice cream from the Italian deli on the corner.

She thinks that being thirteen and the fastest freestyle swimmer in the county is cool, and that girls who only talk about tattoos and reality TV are aliens.

She's someone who doesn't look in the mirror much (unlike her big sister) and hates spending time shopping for clothes, except blue jeans, sweatshirts and trainers, when her old ones have fallen apart.

She thinks best friends will always be there, no matter what.

She believes that each morning the sun will rise, that life is rosy and that strawberry smoothies are the closest thing to heaven.

I suppose you could say I know her pretty well. I should do. The kid is me. And this is my story.

1

I'm standing on the diving block of my local pool in Nottingham, arms extended ahead like a torpedo, head tucked between them, streamlined, muscles taut in anticipation, waiting for the whistle...

I've trained for this race – the under-fourteen girls' 200-metre freestyle – every day for the last three months. The competitor on my right, Mel James, is the current record-holder. She's breathtaking in the water. I've watched her on video and analysed her strokes, searching for the weak points, the areas where I might take advantage.

My coach, Dodgy Dan (on account of his old, beaten-up MG sports car), says it has to be on the turns. That's where I can make up the vital fraction of a second that will make the difference between first and second place.

My heart's thumping in my chest. The crowd is quiet, almost holding its breath. The next two minutes will determine whether I represent the county at the Nationals at Crystal Palace in London later this year. Dad's over there in the stand, probably scratching his ear – he always does that when he's worried about something. Mum's sitting perfectly still, like stone, biting her bottom lip. Even my big sister, Caz, is there somewhere holding my lucky Beanie dog, Dennis (although knowing her, she's on her mobile talking to some boy).

My breathing's a bit tight. Time to give myself a swift talking-to. *Inhale through your nostrils, Amy – fill your lungs slowly. Keep concentrating. Don't let your mind wander.* I can see my reflection in the water. I look like an insect – thin, shimmery, with a shiny head.

'Focus on your pace…' Dan's voice is clear in my head. 'Think about the rhythm of your strokes.'

And there it is at last – the shrill sound of the whistle – a discordant shriek sending impulses through my nervous system, straight to my muscles, asking them to propel me into the air and down into the water like an arrow.

It's a good racing dive, but I can see Mel starting to pull away from me to the surface. I can't afford to let her get a strong lead now. We have to stay neck and neck if I'm not to lose time on the turns.

I'm breaking through the water. The crowd is roaring.

Focus, Amy, cautions my inner voice, the bossy one that usually tells me not to eat crisps and chocolates. *Get the rhythm going. One, two, one, two…*

The girl on my left, Louise Loader, is a good two seconds behind me. I can afford to target all my attention on Mel, whose long legs are powering her effortlessly towards the first turn.

I need to look ahead and judge the number of strokes left between me and the tumble, just like I do every day during training. Dan's wise words echo in my mind. 'It needs to flow, like a single movement.'

One, two, three and down. I flip over and push off the end of the pool, resurfacing. Mel's already there, two strokes ahead. The crowd's roaring louder now – or is it just the rush of blood in my ears? I must lengthen my arms in their sockets and reach into every stroke.

One of my shoulder muscles is aching – I can't have pulled it after all those warm-ups. I must work through the discomfort, make my other arm compensate…

Thirty seconds later and here comes our second turn. I've got to speed up on my recovery. *Tumble more quickly this time, Amy. One, two, three* – Mel's already under the water. Now so am I, turning, reaching up and kicking for all I'm worth.

We're breaking the surface together this time. My chest is hurting. I keep forgetting to breathe out. 'Dummy,' I hear Dan say. 'Let your lungs have a chance…' If I can soften my upper body a little, the pain will ease. My strokes feel suddenly more fluid and fast. I'm working harder than Mel, who is looking relaxed and strong. She's got a great advantage, being five foot five already, and a judo black belt.

Don't think about Mel, idiot! Brain, what are you like? Concentrate on the next tumble and the final fifty metres. Swim as if your life depends on it...

We're turning under the water in complete synchronicity, mirror images of each other. It feels like we're moving in slow motion in a silent world. Now we're on the surface again and people are on their feet, shouting support at us, waving banners, fists clenched in their excitement. All my team members sitting on benches are doing a Mexican wave, back and forth, chanting something. Maybe it's my name! I can't hear anything distinctly, except the pounding of my heart.

The finish is in sight – only twenty-five metres to go. We're neck and neck, each asking our bodies to find that extra bit of energy that will pull us forward towards victory.

Mel's edging ahead. *BREATHE, body, don't let me down now.* I gulp a huge mouthful of air, forcing it down, pushing it out, remembering Dan's drawing of a piston engine. It's working. I'm gaining ground...

Fifteen metres, ten metres, five metres – Mel's fighting back, stretching her hands out, slicing through the foam. Four metres, three metres – *my life depends on this, my life depends on this* – two metres, one metre – *PUSH legs – REACH hands – TOUCH fingers.*

And here it is – the ice-cold feel of the tiles on the pool edge, which my index finger experiences half a second ahead of Mel's. Louise is storming in third, three seconds behind us.

Klaxons are sounding, applause is thundering. My arms are up in the air in a gesture of pure happiness. I can see Mum and Dad holding each other and jumping up and down. Dodgy Dan's giving me the thumbs-up (slightly more dignified). My team's standing on the benches, clapping. I want to remember this moment for the rest of my life. I never want it to end.

'You were fantastic,' I say to Mel, shaking her hand.

She is grasping it and saying 'Well done,' really enthusiastically. I know she must feel crushed. It was so close.

Mel's level of ability and stamina have become my goals and if I'm getting stronger it's largely due to her example and inspiration. I tell her this and she seems pleased.

'Best girl won on the day.' She smiles and adds, 'But watch your back,' as the race official tells us to get out of the pool.

And now the icing on the cake. Over the tannoy, the organisers are announcing that I've set a new record of two minutes and ten seconds for the distance. County champion and record-holder. They're beckoning me to come and stand on the podium and receive my cup and medal. God, I hope I don't blubber.

There's a photographer here from the *County Herald*. For once, I don't care that I'm going to look like a gawky stick insect with biceps in a rubber hat. I've heard other swimmers talk about cloud nine. This must be it.

There's a bit of a commotion nearby. One of the officials has dropped her papers – some of them are in the pool! Sometimes, I know what's going to happen. Scenes flash in front of my eyes. They play in my head like a film reel. I know she's going to bend down to try and pick up the soggy sheets. I've seen her reading glasses fall and heard them smash on the poolside a hundred times before.

Mum says I get it from my gran, this déjà-vu thing. Granny May is half-Irish, and used to read tea leaves, before she lost her marbles. I can't do that, though. We have those pyramid bags, anyway.

The glass fragments are glistening on the water, like shards of ice from a glacier.

A shiver passes down my spine. My body is trembling. Must be the exertion of the race. I wrap my team towel around myself. It feels safe and warm...

2

I'm home at last. The phone's been going non-stop. This time it's Dan for me, says Dad.

'Hi, champ,' says my coach.

'Hi, coach of champ,' I say, mouth full of mozzarella. 'You owe me ten Munch bars.' (This is the unwritten rule when any of Dan's team breaks a county record.)

'Would Madam like them sent round on a silver plate?' he replies and I can hear a wide grin spreading over his bearded face.

'Nah, you can give them to me tomorrow,' I say, coolly.

'You've got tomorrow off, Amy,' he is explaining, and somehow I know what's coming next. 'Training's cancelled. Some idiot's dropped glass in the pool. It's got to be drained…'

I can see the shards glinting, like points of light.

'Cool,' I say, when I really want to shout, 'Wahoo!'

'Enjoy, kiddo,' Dan replies. 'You deserve it.'

And the line goes dead.

So for once, as Saturday-morning light is filtering through my blue curtains, I'm still here in bed at 6 a.m. (I should have remembered to turn my chicken alarm clock off) and 7 a.m. and, WOW, 8 a.m., and now Caz is playing her *Best of Bitch Witch* album next door – loud enough to make the medals on my wall vibrate.

That settles it. I've got the whole day ahead of me. If I want to be a good mate, I could offer to do my best friend, Sophie, a favour and go shopping with her. I'll send her a text, letting her know I'm unexpectedly available. Then I'll have to try and get Caz out of the bathroom. I don't normally have this trouble when I'm training – I'm usually up and gone soon after six.

'Caz,' I whine, banging on the door loudly. 'What are you doing in there?'

'Mind your own business,' comes the reply.

'Need the loo.'

'Go downstairs.'

'Dad's in there and he's been in there for ten minutes so…'

The door opens and Caz's bare arm shoots out clutching a can of air freshener. The rest of her is wrapped in a blue towel. Her face is covered in green slime.

'Use this,' she snaps.

'I need the shower – I'm going out with Sophie.' I'm pleading now.

'Oh my God! You're going shopping? Real shops, not just ones that sell swimsuits?'

That was a bit cutting. 'I think I should mention you are photosynthesising,' I say, sweetly.

Now she's slammed the door and is screaming like a wounded leopard. Fifteen-year-olds are very economical with language. A slam can speak a thousand words. She's probably grinding her teeth too. It's a habit she developed when I was born, apparently, and accounts for her square incisors.

Downstairs, World War Three has broken out. Our dog, Barker, a golden retriever, has been sick on the kitchen floor, having eaten Caz's lipstick last night. (She accused me of stealing it, which is normal. Everything's always my fault.) Anyway, Mum's on the floor with the cloth and the Dettox. Barker is in his basket looking in the other direction, the way he always does when he's denying a crime. Dad's wearing his Mick Jagger pyjamas (a Valentine's present from Mum), covered in big lips.

'Any takers for porridge and cream?' he asks, insensitively.

The visual similarity is too much to bear. I've lost my appetite and can't eat my toast. Normally, I put the crusts in Barker's bowl, but one glance from Mum tells me that he's in big trouble and doesn't deserve any treats. Not now. Not ever.

Dad's sitting next to me, his hair standing up on end like he's a cartoon character. Usually, we would have already been at the pool, Dad timing me with his stopwatch, me sharking up and down, carving a trail in the blue water, slicing some vital tenths of a second off my times. He likes to come and help me at the weekends, and we stop off at Macari's café on the way home for an ice cream or three.

'I could do scrambled eggs…' He still doesn't get it.

The phone's ringing.

'Amy Curtis's personal manager speaking' answers Dad in a stupid voice. He hands me the receiver. 'For you, naturally' he mutters, pretending to be hurt.

'I can't believe you're coming shopping!' Sophie screams, in an ear-piercing shriek.

'Probably a once-in-a-lifetime offer,' I say.

'Mum'll pick you up at nine-thirty. Can you come back for lunch?'

Lunch at the Haynes's is always incredible. Crisps, Pringles, deep-pan pizzas, Coke and ice cream – things we only dream of since Mum became a born-again vegetarian and natural food fanatic.

With her diet in mind, it's a surprise to everyone, and Mum in particular, that Sophie has turned out to be a bit of a distance runner, being 'larger than average' (Mum's words) for her age, and suffering from periodic asthma and an allergy to anything that isn't a convenience food.

Sophie took up running last year and started to shed her extra pounds, and her achievement has inspired both her mum, Shirley, and her ten-year-old brother Gus, who is known to his friends as 'Dollop'. The three of them (they don't talk about Sophie's dad – she calls him

'The Invisible Man') go jogging together.

Shirley wears a yellow plastic flower to tie her long, curly hair back, and sometimes smokes a cigarette. They were invited recently by the local paper to join a 'Fight the Flubber' campaign. Sophie has lost two stone and has become a bit of a celebrity.

I think that's why we're best friends. She knows what it's like to be looked at and recognised in the street and to have parts of her life appear on the front page of the paper on a regular basis. She hates the fact that from the side, she still has two chins. 'It could be worse,' I tell her. At least she's never been photographed with a swimming hat on, looking like a character from *Antz*...

I'm running upstairs, trying to break my record of three seconds from the bottom step to the door of my room, and I'm very excited. We're doing something special this morning. Sophie's saved up for some proper running trainers. Some of the money has come from a feature about her in *Hot Teen* magazine. The rest she's earned doing jobs for her neighbours in the flats, including washing-up, cleaning out budgie cages, that kind of thing. Her mum has given her twenty pounds towards the shoes. They've all had to go without ice cream for a whole month.

Sophie wants to win the 800-metres at Sports Day next week. We've heard that Olivia Brill has got some new jet-propelled running spikes and is having one-to-one coaching to try and win the cup.

My mobile is squawking like an impatient parrot on my bed, telling me I have a message.

'If I'm first over the line,' reads the new text, 'I'll fill the trophy with strawberry smoothie and we'll drink it with giant bendy straws! See you later, alligator.'

I'm imagining this – the flavour of the fruit on my tongue – as Mum knocks on my bedroom door softly, still wearing her rubber gloves, so the knock sounds squelchy. I'm just pulling on my jeans and sweatshirt. I've given up on the shower. By the time Caz finishes in there, the hot water will have run out anyway. Niagara Falls wouldn't be enough for my sister.

'Here,' says Mum, pulling a ten-pound note out of her dressing-gown pocket with yellow rubber fingers. 'Share it with Sophie. Treat yourselves to something nice.'

'Thanks, Mum.' I give her a hug. Not in the way I hug my dad, which is usually violent and involves leaping on him and squeezing him until he can't breathe, while taking both my feet off the ground. (Mum is more sensitive than Dad and hates loud noise, violent hugging and icky things like dog's vomit. She is a painter and says she likes canvases because they don't speak, except to the imagination. I don't really get that, but she says I will when I am older.)

I've already decided I will treat Sophie and myself to strawberry smoothies with extra cream and marshmallows once she is the proud owner of an ice-white, hundred-pound pair of marathon trainers with go-faster stripes.

'She's here,' shouts Dad in his Baloo voice. God, he's opening the door in his big-lips pyjamas. And he's singing 'I'm the King of the Swingers' with his face puckered up, like he's in pain. Luckily, Sophie is used to my dad and just nods sadly at him. I kiss him on the cheek on my way out and he does this soppy-bear smile.

Once we're through the door, Sophie dances about on the path like a maniac. She grabs me and we spin round and round, nearly falling into the flower beds. The last time we did this, Sophie had just come top in the end-of-year religious studies exam. 'That's just frigging fantastic.' her mum had said. 'My Sophie's going to become a priest.'

'Wahoo!' shouts Sophie. 'Today is the best day of my life so far.'

'Didn't realise going shopping with me was so exciting,' I reply. Soph's really hyper today. Maybe she had chocolate spread for breakfast.

Shirley's waiting in the car – a blue estate that smells strongly of sickly-sweet oranges. She's wearing two blue hair braids and a T-shirt that says 'Dream on'.

Now Dad's doing this impression of a nodding dog out of the lounge window, to mimic the one on the back shelf of Sophie's car. He's embarrassing sometimes, my dad.

'He's a one, isn't he?' says Shirley, waving at him.

I just say 'yeah' because I'm always careful to stay off the 'dad' subject for obvious reasons. And it's all right to say 'yeah' to Sophie's mum, whereas my mum would insist on 'yes'. The Beatles always said 'yeah', though, and they were cool.

Gus is hunched up on the back seat, the remains of his chocolate-coated cereal round his mouth. A grubby baseball cap is perched the wrong way round on his head. He smells of chips.

'I'll get in the back with him,' says Sophie, pulling a face. 'Shove up,' she tells her brother.

Gus grins at me shyly. His small blue eyes almost disappear into his round cheeks as he does so.

'Hello, Dollop,' I say, to be friendly. It's hard not to stare at the red, flaking skin under his nostrils.

''lo, Ame,' he replies, sniffing. His nose and throat always sound blocked. Mum thinks he's allergic to dairy products. Shirley blames the damp in their flat. She says that's why he always cuts words in half…

'Don't worry. He's going to Splodger's house for lunch,' Sophie reassures me.

''ving lasaggie,' Gus informs us, licking his lips with his tongue and rubbing his stomach. I'm aware his eyes haven't left me once since I got in the car.

'What's lasaggie when it's at home?' asks Shirley.

'Do you mean lasagne, Dollop?' I ask.

'Ha, ha, ha,' replies Dollop, so I take that as a 'yes'.

Sophie waves a wad of twenty-pound notes at me excitedly.

'Could buy ten guinea piggles for that,' says Gus, quietly. 'Stupid shoes.'

'They're not stupid shoes,' snaps Sophie. 'These will be the whitest, fastest, coolest, trendiest trainers on the planet.' She pulls her eyelids up and sticks her tongue out at Gus, who copies her. It's not a pretty sight. They look like two gargoyles.

'Mind the wind doesn't change,' warns Shirley, glancing in her rear-view mirror. She winks at me, a smile creasing round her eyes.

'Red alert, red alert, we're passing the pool!' shouts Sophie suddenly, hands on my shoulders, restraining me. I pretend to struggle. 'You need to have a life outside Lycra,' she bosses.

So, we pass the pool and I don't leap out and do an SAS roll or anything, but I do realise my left shoulder is quite stiff. That always happens on the rare occasions when I don't train. Things seize up. My body's a finely tuned machine that needs a lot of maintenance, including professional massage and high-protein food. Poor Mum has to sacrifice her new principles several times a week and cook me meat. My coach says my muscles need it for their development. Mum often closes her eyes and apologises to whichever animal it was she's cutting into cubes.

'I'm really sorry about this, little lamb. I hope you had

a nice time frolicking in the field with your mum before they loaded you onto that frightening truck...'

I know every inch of my body – the bits that are strong, those that are weak. From the back, I look like a triangle with measles, Caz says, as my shoulders are broadening and becoming blotchy. Mum blames the chlorine and my hormones, which are starting to party.

At least a bit of me is having a social life.

I've got used to the training, seven days a week. It's a way of life – a journey towards a final goal, which for most athletes is ultimately the Olympics. When I'm racing, I'm filled with excitement and adrenaline, a chemical which Dan says your body releases when you need to act quickly. Even in Sophie's car, on this busy Saturday morning, I can imagine the vibration of my competitors either side of me and hear the combined noise of people cheering us on. I am, in Caz's words, 'addicted' to swimming.

It's an incredible feeling, winning a race. Those moments have kept me going through two years of relentless training. I want to feel that way again and again. I dream that one day, I'll stand on the tall podium in some faraway place and listen to the national anthem and take home a gold medal for Britain.

I want Sophie to have that feeling too, after winning the 800-metres at Sports Day.

That's why I'm here in the centre of Nottingham, in

some shoe shop, buying trainers with my best friend, who can't stop smiling as she's trying on about four million pairs. We've been in here an hour now. White shoes festoon the floor like flakes of snow. The shop assistant is looking really tetchy. She has developed a twitch in her right eye every time she looks at Gus, who is lying on the floor, buried under empty shoeboxes, making guinea-pig noises.

Sophie finally decides on a pair. 'Do you like them, Amy?' she keeps asking me.

''Course I like them,' I reply, maybe a dozen times.

'What do you like most about them, then?'

'The stripes.'

'You don't think they're too...stripy?'

'No.'

'I would have liked blue stripes more,' she says. We all groan.

'The colour of the stripes won't make you faster,' I point out. 'Silver is really cool, and with a bit of luck, they'll dazzle Olivia as you storm past her on the final bend and take first place.'

'Supposing she beats me by miles,' she says, eyes downcast.

Time to talk tough. 'You can't think like that. You have to fix your eyes on the finishing line, focus on your pace and GO FOR IT.'

'I'm not very good at the focusing bit. If I start thinking about my pace, I fall over,' she admits.

'The go-for-it bit is the most important,' I tell her.

'It's Amy's Law. Right, Coach?' She grins at me and suddenly gives me a massive hug.

'Yeah, if you like,' I agree, flattered.

'Maybe I should have got spikes…'

Shirley decides at this point that she needs more cigarettes and it seems the right time to suggest a trip to the Pink Flamingo café opposite. Shirley tells us to use the crossing and she and Gus will meet us inside in a minute.

The street is crowded with families buying clothes in the July sales – T-shirts to take on holiday, paddling pools for back gardens parched by weeks of sun. Everyone's smiling, or looking like they are, in the sunshine.

'Do you see who I see?' I say to Sophie, pointing ahead.

It's two boys from our year at school. They are nudging each other and pointing at us.

'Hello, Hot Stuff,' calls Sophie, waving. Peter Furnace goes a bright shade of pink, which looks seriously bad against his ginger hair. His weasly mate, Dom, is creasing up. Hot Stuff is walking towards us, his hands in his pockets, trying to look cool.

'Hey,' he says, looking at us, then back at Dom, then at the ground.

'Hey, Hot Stuff,' says Sophie.

'Saw you. In my sister's magazine,' he mutters, glancing at her almost reverently.

'Is that the one of me with four chins?' asks Sophie, laughing, squashing her chin back against her throat and holding a pose.

'Yeah. I mean, no. You were wearing a blue thing. A ponko.'

'I looked a right idiot, didn't I?' nods Soph, suppressing giggles, choosing not to tell her admirer that actually, it was a poncho.

'Could I…have your autograph?' asks Hot Stuff, as red as a tomato now.

'Sure,' says Sophie. 'Got a pen?'

He looks crestfallen. 'Nah. I've got me arm, though,' he says, rolling up his sleeve to reveal a pale, freckly limb.

'I'll use my eyeliner,' says Sophie, rummaging in her bag and producing a dark kohl, which she uses on photo shoots and wouldn't be seen dead in otherwise.

Hot Stuff looks at his signed arm proudly. It reads, 'To Hot Stuff. Love, Sophie xxx.' He is beaming at her.

'Um. Can I snog you?'

'God, no,' says Sophie, shocked. Dom is sniggering behind Hot Stuff.

'Your loss,' he says, shrugging sadly and walking away, holding his arm as if it is a precious gift.

We're waiting at the crossing and Soph is kissing the box in her arms and telling the trainers she loves them. I wonder if Hot Stuff is watching…

'I'm going to buy you the biggest strawberry smoothie

you have ever seen,' I promise. Her eyes widen with pleasure.

'Just one thing,' she says, holding my arm. 'I need something BAD on top.'

'Squirty cream?' I whisper.

'And chocolate flakes and sprinkles and...'

'Marshmallows.'

We check the road and step out onto the zebra stripes. I glance at Sophie and see her angel-blonde hair glinting in the sunlight, her mouth wide open, giggling, her round face radiant and beautiful. She has never looked more happy. And beyond this, somewhere in the distance, a large, dark shape is looming like an eclipse.

I've been here before, in my nightmares ...

And suddenly, there's an ear-splitting, whistling noise, like fifty camping kettles boiling at the same time, and a terrible screeching of metal sparking against metal, and there is angel hair in my face and white sunlight shafting into my eyes like swords.

And now everything is black. I feel as if I'm swimming underwater, somewhere very cold and very dark – a faraway ocean – and I'm alone and frightened. And there is no sound. Not even the slightest echo of her laughter.

3

Dad, I'm scared.

Perhaps I am asleep and when I wake up, I will be in my bed at home, warm and safe, eyes tight shut, waiting for the shrill sound of the cock-a-doodle-doo alarm clock at 5.30 a.m.

Mum, hold me please.

Perhaps I'm dead. Doomed to swim for ever in a black, soulless ocean. No, I can't buy that. I've always been kind to animals (the ones I'm not eating for training purposes) and old people, like Joan next door, who has arthritis and can't bend down without farting. I haven't had time to get my head round the God thing, so maybe this is where people go who haven't signed up to anything.

If this is eternity, I don't think I want to stay here long…

Mum says it's up to all of us to make up our own minds about religion. She describes herself as 'spiritual'. Dad says he's into spirits as well, particularly single malts.

I can see images of my family in this place, but when I reach out to them, they fade away. Dad looks like he's praying right now, so he must be really into it. Caz is more of a Buddhist, putting flowers by a shrine with my picture inside. I can see Shirley, standing nude in the rain in the night, with her arms lifted up to the moon. Mum says she's a pagan. I had to look that up, and the dictionary said they worship spirits of the wind, earth and sky. I quite like that idea. Dad says it's an excuse to get her kit off. That's the first unkind thing I've ever heard him say…

Weird how I can picture them all, and feel their pain, in my darkness…I imagine I can hear them speaking, but their voices are like whispers on a passing wind.

Mum's saying it's her fault – if she hadn't given me that ten-pound note, none of it would have happened.

Shirley is blaming herself – if she hadn't gone to get that 'stupid packet of fags', she would have seen it coming.

Dad, please help me. Bring me home…

Dad is beating himself up because he thought about taking me to another pool to train – so I would never have been on the crossing at all. And probably, at that moment, neither would Sophie.

Gus is asking if he can buy a guinea pig…

My sister is saying none of it is her fault, although if I get the chance, I will point out that if she hadn't taken an hour in the bathroom, we might have left sooner and therefore crossed the road at a different time. This won't be a popular suggestion.

Strangely, the driver of the lorry blames the person on the end of the phone he was holding to his ear when he ran us over.

I won't ever forgive you...

Blame is an interesting thing. It seems to bring out the worst in people. And it doesn't change the reality of what has happened. Calling it 'the accident' is more comfortable for everyone, because that way, no one is to blame. It is an act of God. (Ha! So technically, it's God's fault.)

I could blame strawberry smoothies. They should carry a government health warning. 'Do not cross the road for this drink. Smoothies can kill.'

I'm afraid. I can't feel my body. Sophie, are you there?

I think God, like blame, means different things to different people. And there is no right and wrong about it. In fact, the idea of God is so huge that whole continents rely on a book full of rules, which they say is the word of God. So how come there are different books with different rules, depending on where you live? Does that mean there are different gods? How do you know which is the best one? And how do you know that the rules weren't made up by people a long time ago? (That's what Mum believes.)

I can feel panic rising like a tidal wave, gathering strength, gaining momentum, sucking me up into its monumental mass...

In this dark place, I know that whatever God is, it's a feeling thing, not a book thing. And I don't feel dead. On the other hand, I don't feel very alive either. Whichever way I turn, there is darkness. Even in the deepest ocean, light filters down to certain depths. As hard as I try to swim upwards, the blackness never becomes blue. No way out, brain. We're defeated.

And the wave is breaking, rolling me over and over, filling my lungs with fluid, crushing me with its force. I feel nothing, except a faint vibration, like a distant drumbeat, on and on. Perhaps it is my heart.

Or a memory of my heart.

I haven't heard the voices of my family for the longest time. I am even forgetting what they sound like. Maybe I will forget who I am and will just drift through this underworld into oblivion.

How long have I been here? No one can answer that.

Time is so important in my life – I'm always clock-watching, making sure I get everything done so that I can get to training. In this place, there is no such thing as time management. I am an irrelevance. My desires are of no consequence. I have given myself up to time. It is managing me.

The vibrations are getting more insistent. And there's a muffled noise like an old wizard coughing.

Did you hear me, God? I think I need to keep an open mind about you...

Some people believe you can be born lots of times. Is that what is happening to me now? Soph and I talked about this last week in maths, and she said she'd like to come back as my sister, and I said it probably doesn't work like that and that next time, we could be pigs – and she oinked and got us both a detention.

Perhaps I'm being drawn slowly down to the engine at the centre of the earth that recycles souls and I am about to be born again to a new family in an unfamiliar part of the world.

I haven't said goodbye to Mum and Dad… I'm not ready to leave them. I want to stay, I want to feel them holding me and hear them laughing.

You can't make me go if I'm not ready, whatever you are, whoever you are. I'm Amy Curtis and I need to go home…

I have a strange sensation in my chest – it feels like anger. And I'm in motion, doing breaststroke, I think. Far above me, there is white light, lying on top of the black, like an Irish coffee. I'm getting nearer and the black is merging into blue – and the blue into tropical turquoise.

Are there dolphins here? I've always wanted to swim with dolphins…

The water is warm now and my chest is loosening after the effort of swimming so hard. With just a little more effort, I can break the surface and see the sun…

My eyes are taking in the dazzling brightness and acclimatising to the air, and I can see…

'Oh my God!' splutters Caz, staring at me, part of a banana protruding from her open mouth.

'You look thinner,' I want to say, but can't, as there is something hard down my throat. I lift my fingers of my right hand and give her a wave, which seems to upset her, as she starts to cry.

'Hey, baby, it's good to have you back,' sing the Furballs on the CD player Caz is clutching on her lap.

4

'Barker was here,' says Caz, sobbing. 'I recorded him barking so that you would hear him.'

The wizard with a cough.

'And I've been playing all your favourite CDs.'

So Caz has been my astral angel, bringing me back from the edge of doom in a black universe. With a little help from the doctors and nurses. 'And Mum and Dad,' says Caz. They have taken it in turns to change my tubes and empty my waste bags, stroke my hands and wash my face. I can't imagine how boring it must have been for them, sitting by my bed, day after day, night after night, watching the monitor for signs of movement.

I've been in a coma for ten days.

And suddenly, this room is full of people. Mum, Dad, medics – and there are lots of tears. The tube that has been helping me breathe is taken out of my throat, which now feels very dry and sore. Mum and Dad are holding me, but they're not laughing like in the vision I had in my dark place. They both look grey, like ghosts, and Mum hasn't brushed her hair. Dad's gone native and has given up shaving. His bristles scratch my face when he kisses me.

I keep saying it's OK because I'm back now, so they can stop worrying.

Dad's looking at the ceiling and saying 'thank you' so he has probably lost his marbles, unless he's discovered a new religion that involves worshipping light bulbs...

When I say I'm back, that's not quite true. I feel like I'm inside a bubble, watching things happen around me. Reality fades in and out. I'm not reacting to things in the way I would expect. It's as if my brain and my heart aren't connected. I want to ask lots of questions, but can't find the words.

The doctors say that's because I'm in shock.

'You stopped breathing on your own for a long time,' says Caz, in my ear. 'The consultant told Mum and Dad your brain was swollen and you were probably going to die. Mum told her you definitely weren't and sat next to you, talking to you non-stop for about five days. They say you're a miracle kid.'

Go, Mum.

The room is emptying a bit now. Caz is waving at me from the doorway. Maybe that's just my eyes playing tricks. A nurse has an arm round her because she seems a bit wobbly. Now it's just Mum and Dad and a woman in a white coat with a bun and metal-rimmed glasses, and the door is closed and the bubble is closing in. My eyelids are droopy. I must stay awake. If I go to sleep, I might go back to the dark place.

Mum is holding my hand. Dad is holding Mum. I think the news must be bad. I must have had a transplant. They've taken out my heart. That's why I can't feel anything… But your heart is supposed to go on, no matter what. That's what Jack told Rose in *Titanic*.

Dad's face is puckering up, like when he's singing karaoke. Tears are squeezing out of his eyes and running down his cheeks. As fast as he is wiping them away, more are coming. His chest is rising and falling sharply. I've never seen my dad cry before. My eyes are filling up in sympathy, although I don't know what I am reacting to.

'…significant advances in prosthetic lower limbs, which will make it possible to walk and lead a normal life.' The doctor is speaking to me. None of her words are making sense. Mum is holding my hand tighter. Hers is trembling.

'I'm sorry, I don't understand…' I tell the doctor. (My voice sounds uncannily like Yoda's.) No point her waffling on if it's not sinking in. 'What's happened to me?'

The doctor is looking at Mum, who reaches forward and gently pushes my hair off my forehead.

'You were knocked down on the crossing,' begins Mum, still stroking my hair. She's shaking her head and doesn't want to say anything else.

The doctor is taking off her glasses. Her dark eyes are much prettier without them. 'It was a serious accident, Amy,' she is saying. 'You are a very lucky girl to be here, a very strong girl. The swelling in your brain caused by your fall is now responding well to treatment. Unfortunately, your right leg was badly damaged below the knee, and we couldn't save it.'

I feel sick. Her words are spinning in my consciousness. For the first time, I notice the raised tent at the end of my bed. I lift the sheet and stare south. My left leg is bruised and swollen, like a black jelly baby. My toes are waving back at me cheerfully, like old friends. My right leg appears to stop after the knee, which is stumpy with bandages. I blink and focus again. It's not an optical illusion. Part of me is missing. A vital part…

'So I can't swim…' The words choke out of my constricted throat.

Dad is making strange, sobbing noises. I feel so faint…

Mum anticipates what's going to happen next and is ready with the bedpan, just as I start retching.

'How…?' is all I manage, before I start shaking violently and the doctor gives me an injection in my arm and suddenly, I feel calm again and the room is full of flowers and I am floating in a multicoloured sky, somersaulting, back-flipping in slow motion. But in this amazing space, I have both my legs. I can feel them both moving…

5

I've opened my eyes. I'm in the same room as earlier, except now it's night and the only light is outside in the hospital corridor and on the machines I'm wired up to, which bleep every so often. My right hand is sore where the drip needle is attached, delivering fluid into my dehydrated body.

My chest is tightening up as I look at the tent over my bed. Over where my whole right leg used to be. My fingers clench and I want to yell. I've never felt so angry. I didn't say they could take my leg away – my poor, shattered limb. They didn't even give it a chance. God, I'm going to blubber now. I can feel it coming.

And there's something else – something I need to know. It's a question that isn't quite taking shape in my brain. It's about Sophie…

'Mum,' I whisper.

Mum's here, asleep in a chair. She looks about fourteen – small and vulnerable. But Mum is stronger than all of us, even though she's only five foot three. We were joined once, all those years ago. I feel part of her again, wrapped in the power of her love. Maybe it's the lifeline that is keeping me alive.

'Hey,' she says, opening her eyes quickly. So she was

only pretending to be asleep, just in case she let me go, accidentally.

'How long…?' I can't finish the sentence. I'm confused about what should come next. I can't remember the past tense of 'sleeping'. My brain is full of fog. My voice is croaky. I now sound like the Wicked Witch of the West from *The Wizard of Oz*.

'About eight hours,' she replies, coming and sitting next to the bed. 'Would you like a drink?'

'Gin and tonic,' I say, managing a grin. The anger is passing.

'Coming right up,' she replies, pouring a glass of water and holding it to my lips. I take a sip and feel it travel all the way to my stomach.

I notice that on my bedside table, next to several get-well cards, there is a framed photo of Barker, holding a ball on the end of a rope – his favourite toy.

'He sends his love,' says Mum. 'And asked me to tell you that he misses you very much.'

'I heard him,' I smile. 'In my faraway place.'

'You started breathing on your own again when Caz played the CD of him barking,' she tells me, stroking my hair.

'He helped retrieve me,' I say, holding Mum's hand. I feel safer now.

'The first useful thing he's ever done.' She grins, but her eyes are moist and red-rimmed.

'I hope you gave him a big biscuit as a reward.' I smile.

'I bought him a new white-and-blue collar. He's on a diet,' Mum replies and we laugh.

'Sorry – about all this,' I say and my lip is suddenly wobbling.

Mum sits on the bed and hugs me, rocking me backwards and forwards, like she used to when I fell off my first bike.

'You have nothing to be sorry about,' she tells me, and there is anger in her voice. 'There are those who should be sorry. For the rest of their lives. But you are my beautiful girl, who has come back to me. And you must never, never apologise for that.'

And then the words that have been tormenting my subconscious escape my mouth before my brain has a chance to protect me from the variety of answers that could follow.

'What about Sophie?'

Mum releases me from the hug and is gathering herself up to speak. In the half-light, I can see her mouth opening, then closing again. Silence.

'Mum? I want to know.'

'Sophie's gone – to the other place.'

I nod. Shock waves zap through every cell of my being. Something in my head screams, 'No!' My friend has left me forever. Best friends are supposed to do everything together...

We sit, Mum and I, for ages without saying another word. Mum is watching me, ready to minister to whatever reaction comes first. I feel blank, like an empty canvas, devoid of colour. My machines bleep to indicate signs of life. Somewhere in the corridor outside, someone is pushing a trolley with a squeaky wheel.

And suddenly I can hear metal on metal and the sun is being obliterated by a black monster bearing down on us and Sophie is falling against me and then...nothing. I gasp and my body goes rigid for a moment, as the memory courses through my bloodstream. Mum holds my arms firmly.

'You're safe now, Amy. I'm here,' she keeps repeating, until my breathing calms. I've broken out in a sweat. Mum moistens a tissue with water from the jug and wipes my forehead softly. I want to cry so much, but this new loss is beyond grief. My smashed-up body trembles in ripples, like smooth water disturbed by a sharp stone.

Twenty minutes pass. I can feel the pulse of the seconds in my brain. The pain in my chest is so intense I can't speak.

'Who won the 800-metres?' is the first thing I say, eventually, pointlessly, suddenly remembering Sports Day.

'It was cancelled,' Mum soothes. 'Shirley invited everyone to Sophie's funeral.'

I'm taking this in. My friend has had her funeral while I've been unconscious. I wasn't even there to say goodbye.

'She wore her running kit, including her new trainers,' continues Mum, stroking my hand. 'School's going to name the Athletics Cup after her.'

Too much information, Mum. My brain's on overload. I can see Sophie in a box in her stupid trainers. 'She didn't even get a chance to use them,' I say, bitterly.

Mum is rummaging in her handbag. 'Shirley asked me to give you this,' she says, holding something in her hand. It's a silver teddy on a chain. Sophie's lucky charm. I was with her the day she hooked a duck and won it at the fair. It's the one she wears when she is racing. Only it's not very lucky, as it turns out.

I hold it in my hand and hope that somehow it will bring Sophie close again. It's cold, like a small piece of ice. The teddy's eyes are fixed in an empty stare. I stare back. I can't get Sophie's bear thing. She has dozens of them arranged round her room, glassy eyes empty and lifeless. 'Aw, look,' she always says when we see a sad, furry face in a shop window. 'He needs rescuing.' And five minutes later, another teddy is starting a new life in Sophie's care.

'I'll pay you back,' she says, every time.

'Yeah, yeah,' I shrug.

And I am suddenly overwhelmed by something unexpected and unfamiliar – guilt.

'I should have gone with her. Best friends give up everything for each other,' I suddenly blurt out, and the dam in my brain breaks and saltwater pours through my eyes and nose. 'I shouldn't have let her go on her own…'

Mum is enveloping me. I can smell lavender in her jumper. My closed eyes see rolling purple fields in French sunlight. And a child, with angel hair, running through them.

6

'Hey, Amy,' says Dad, a falsely cheerful smile on his face. 'How's Trix?'

'Surviving,' I reply, truthfully.

He kisses my forehead and slumps down on the chair next to me. He's wearing his cream shirt with green palm trees on and his old jeans. It must be Saturday.

'Oh,' he says, reaching into his jeans pocket. 'Messages from Dan and the team. They want to come and see you as soon as you're up to it.'

He hands me the crumpled paper, which has lots of writing on it in different-coloured ink. The words blur together and make flower patterns in front of my eyes.

'How's your head?' asks Dad gently.

'Feels weird,' I admit. 'Like it belongs to someone else.'

'Have you looked in the mirror to make sure?' he teases. I never want to look in the mirror again. I'm trying not to cry.

'Always say the wrong...' Dad rubs his face with his hands roughly.

'It's OK, Dad,' I try to reassure him.

'I wasn't there for you,' he whispers, his voice cracking.

'Here now,' I say. 'All that matters.'

I hold out my hand and he takes it in his, squeezing it hard.

'I don't know why things like this have to happen,' he says, searching my face for an answer. I just shake my head. Tears have fought their way out of my eyes and onto my cheeks. There are no answers. Only questions, mostly starting with 'What if…?'

'Doing a great job of cheering you up, eh?' he smiles, his eyes red with sadness.

'Got any jokes?' I say, knowing he has millions, even if I've heard them all before. He brightens suddenly.

'What do you call a man floating in the water?'

This is one of my favourites. It's so silly I always end up on the floor holding my stomach. If only I could remember how it goes…

'Starts with a "B",' he says encouragingly.

'B, b, b…' And then it comes to me. 'Bob!' I blurt out, a grin spreading from ear to ear.

'And what do you call a man with a spade in his head?'

Come on, Amy, get into gear…

'Doug,' I respond, and we both laugh, mostly with relief that my brain hasn't completely lost its sense of humour.

'You're a great girl, Amy, you know that, don't you?' says Dad, holding my gaze.

'Uh-huh,' I answer, as upbeat as possible. The truth is, I'm in free fall and I don't know how the pieces are going to fit together when they land.

And now Dad's leaving, saying something about getting to B&Q before it closes for some teak oil for the garden furniture. The palm trees are swaying in a tropical breeze, and before I know it, I'm staring at the insides of my eyelids and sinking into a black silence.

～

It's the middle of the night. I must have missed Mum visiting because there's a note from her saying, 'Sleep tight, mind the slugs don't bite xx', which is what she used to say when I was little and afraid of the light being turned off. We would argue about whether slugs had teeth or not and I would forget to be frightened.

I wish she were here now, with her arms round me, telling me about her day and what Barker's been up to. I wouldn't even mind if Caz arrived and starting moaning about her latest boy problems. Anything would be better than hearing the hum of the machines monitoring whether or not my blood pressure is going to go through the roof and make me explode into a thousand fragments.

My left hand is aching where the drip needle is attached. Fluid and painkillers are seeping into my soul like stealthy burglars in soft shoes, spreading out to case the joint and overwhelm any resistance with quiet force.

I should just pull them out – all these wires. At least then the pain would be real and I could stop thinking and start reacting. I'm numb, in a surreal place that smells of pine needles and poo.

I almost died. That's what they said. I should be grateful, optimistic, glad. But I'm in mourning, because the Amy who was is gone forever. The lorry killed her dreams and turned her heart to stone. I'm wearing an invisible veil of black.

They dragged me back from the Other Place to inhabit this broken body and live a spectator's life, surrounded by searing cheers and clanging applause. All I can do now is gaze into the calm, inviting, beautiful world beneath the water, where weight is suspended and existence is measured in bubbles…where resistance does a magical thing to movement, turning it into ballet. And where everything flows – energy, thoughts, hopes, dreams… I've left my whole self down there, in that space below the surface.

Maybe, if my geeky physics teacher, Mr Jupitus, is right, and there is a parallel universe in which we carry on living life as we were, I'm there still – the Amy Curtis of just a few days ago, in my perfect world, somewhere deeper than blue.

Most of us think Mr Jupitus is two electrons short of an atom, so that concept is no comfort at this moment.

So I hate them – the doctors who patched me up, the ones who pop in and tell me I will lead a 'full life', the nurses who smile at me sweetly all day. I hate Caz for reaching out into my darkness and reeling me in – a strange fish on a foreign shore, with the hook tearing at its gaping mouth. I hate Mum and Dad for being selfish and wanting me back at all costs, just so that they can carry on loving me.

I hate myself because I am full of hate. Not to be would be easier.

Mum has left her cardigan on the chair, the cerise-pink one with a wavy hem. I can just reach it. I cover my face with it and breathe deeply. It smells of lavender conditioner and Mum's daytime perfume.

I could make this pain stop forever.

It would be possible to put the sleeves around my neck and tie them to the top of the metal bedstead. I would only have to lean forward. It would be like that game when you hold your breath for as long as possible when you go through a tunnel. Nothing to be scared of. And you can decide not to play at any time.

The sleeves are soft on my skin. The label says the cardigan is a mix of angora and wool. Dad couldn't wear anything like that – much too itchy. Mum's fine with natural fibres. No surprises there.

Dad taught me how to tie knots from a special book on sailing. It's not easy doing it with one hand, though. Nearly impossible, if you must know. Sweat beads are forming above my eyes with the effort of it. OK. One more loop under, round and back. It's done. I'll do a quick test run just to see if it's able to bear my weight. I lower my neck and rest it in the apex of the cardigan. I feel cradled. It's like coming home.

God, one of the arms has unknotted. There is an alternative. I could just wrap the sleeves round my neck and keep pulling.

You can only take a life when there is a life to take. *Sorry Mum. I know how you love this cardigan...*

'Amy, are you feeling chilly?' Sister Beresford, a short, plump nurse with a round, open face, is suddenly at my bedside ramming a thermometer into my mouth. She seems very concerned. I must look like a rabbit caught in headlights. She takes my pulse and stares into my face.

The thermometer reads 103 degrees. I must have been dreaming again...

'You're sweating,' she sighs. 'I'll get you some ice and see if we can increase your meds.' She takes the cardigan from my hands and folds it neatly on the chair by the door, leaving her hand on it for a moment longer than necessary.

'It's a lovely pink,' she says quietly. 'Like a winter sunset.'

7

'There are three things you should know about the Amputee Club,' says a confident voice on my right. 'One, people think you have lost your faculties and speak to you very slowly. Two, they try not to laugh in your presence in case you get angry with them because they're not stumpy. Three, no one will buy you a skirt or a pair of shorts for Christmas.'

I open my eyes and take in the sight of a ward full of different-sized children in ordered beds and a long mural on the wall opposite showing a flying bee smiling down on sunflowers in a field, their upturned faces beaming at the sky. Inside an arcing rainbow are painted the words 'Sunflower Ward'. They must have moved me out of my private space in the night...

'You deaf or something?' continues the voice, slightly annoyed. I turn to see a thin boy of about fourteen with a pale face and lips and dark eyes with long lashes. He is wearing checked pyjamas two sizes too big and a Davy Crockett racoon hat on his head.

'You talking to me?' I say, staring at the stripy brown tail at the back of his neck.

'Ralph.' He grins.

'Hello Ralph,' I reply, coolly.

'No, the hat's Ralph. I'm Harry. Harry Higgins.'

'Amy Curtis,' I say. Harry looks like he wants to shake hands, but there's too much of a gap between our beds.

'No make friends with this naughty boy,' cautions a deep voice from the direction of my left foot. A small, skinny woman with black hair in a loose plait and large eyes like a baby fawn is smiling at me. She has a plastic apron on and is holding a mop in both hands.

'You look gorgeous this morning, Isabella' says Harry.

The woman blushes. 'You cheeky, Harry Higgins,' she replies, shaking the mop pole at him. The 'Harry' sounds like 'Haaaa-ri' – almost musical. 'He give you any trouble, you call Isabella,' she says to me, before returning to her work, mopping rhythmically between the beds, her face wearing a look of determination to wipe out all germs.

'Isabella's good for a wind-up,' says Harry quietly. 'She's from Barcelona. And she's promised to teach me the tango…'

I can feel myself starting to like this kid. I notice two false lower legs standing to attention on the other side of his bed.

Harry shrugs, following my gaze. 'Had a bit of cosmetic surgery. My legs were puny rubbish so I swapped them for some new ones.' He smiles, revealing two rows of small, perfect teeth.

'What really happened?' I hear myself asking. 'Sorry,' I add quickly, 'you may not want to…'

'Caught meningitis – that brain thing – and my blood went weird and septic. They couldn't save my legs.'

'That's awful,' I mutter, wishing I could think of something that didn't sound so pathetic.

'Good thing is the scans showed I had something the size of an orange growing in my spine and if I hadn't had the brain trouble, they'd never have known about Trevor.'

'Trevor?'

'My tumour. That's what I call him. Swedish researchers say if you talk to your tumour, you can make it go away. They're big on the power of positive thinking.'

'Do you live in hospital?' I ask, a dozen questions jostling in my head.

'Nah. Just here temporarily for the free drugs and social life.' Harry winks. 'Like to keep them on their toes. Some days, my blood count's up, so I can have chemo – the stuff they pump in to kill the cancer cells. Some days it's down. Sister Beresford secretly thinks I'm just attention-seeking, although she always puts her head on one side and tells me I'm "lovely".' Harry demonstrates, fluttering his eyelashes.

I open my mouth but no words come.

Harry senses my discomfort and points to the open magazine on his lap. 'My dream machine.' He holds up the glossy double pages showing a state-of-the-art wheelchair. 'Spangly, don't you think?'

'Spangly?'

'Fantastic. Coolio… Like Nurse Emmerson.' Harry points to a pretty nurse with long legs at the end of our ward. 'And him.' He nods to the picture of Barker on my bedside table.

'It must cost a lot,' I say, impressed with the gleaming chrome, chunky grab handles and streamlined shape. I realise I've never looked closely at a wheelchair before.

'I won't need one for much longer, hopefully. Not once the chemo is finished. Then I'm going to buy a Porsche.' Harry grins at me.

'Yeah, right,' I say. 'Although maybe a helicopter would be better.'

'That's just stupid. They're a nightmare to park.' He is still grinning at me.

'Harry, are they going to take your tumour out?' I can't believe I just asked him that. I deserve a real mouthful…

'Too near my heart – too dangerous,' replies Harry simply. 'We're working on shrinking Trevor and blasting him into extinction, like in *Star Wars*.' Harry enacts a fight scene with a pretend light sabre. 'The Force is with me.'

I'm nodding, not wanting to remind Harry that a light sabre wasn't enough to protect Obi-Wan Kenobi.

'So. What's your story, then?' asks Harry lightly, still looking at his spangly machine.

I'm not sure where to begin.

A small blond boy wearing glasses, dirty jeans and a sweatshirt is trundling a bag of fluid on wheels past the end of my bed. The bag is attached to the boy's hand via a transparent tube.

'Small Fry! Result!' calls Harry, clapping. The boy called Small Fry gives a toothless grin.

'Thankth for thoth anitheed twithts, Harry,' he says, and blushes, moving down the ward, unsteady but determined, wiping his running nose on his sleeve.

'Pneumonia,' whispers Harry. 'His dad made him sleep in the shed with the dog. He's got a foster family now.'

I take this in and wonder how many of the other twelve children on Sunflower Ward have terrible tales to tell. Harry is staring at me intently, eyebrows raised.

I haven't said it out loud before. 'Lost my right leg.' That wasn't so bad.

'Details?' asks Harry, softly.

'Zebra crossing.'

'Car?' he persists.

'Lorry.'

'Ouch.'

'Yeah.'

'Still here, though.' He nods, holding my gaze. 'Survivors, you and me.'

'My friend Sophie...' I can't finish. My throat has closed up.

Harry takes this in and reaches into the drawer of his bedside table, rummaging around impatiently. He produces a bag of assorted mini chocolate bars and throws half a dozen at me in succession.

'Eat these immediately. It's an order. Your blood sugar is dropping.'

I unwrap a caramel bar reluctantly and put it in my mouth. My tongue responds eagerly – ignoring my brain telling it this is not the time for selfish indulgence.

Harry is watching me closely. 'Good,' he says. 'That's very good.'

I give him the thumbs-up and carry on chewing.

'Like I was saying,' he says, 'when you were ignoring me. There are three things you should know about this exclusive club of ours...'

8

'How are you feeling today, Amy?' asks Nurse Emmerson, who is checking my leg bandages. White curtains separate us from the rest of the ward.

'Fine,' I reply. 'A bit sleepy.'

'That'll be the painkillers working,' she soothes, in her soft Scottish accent. 'Your mum's here, by the way.'

Actually, Mum's outside in the hospital garden, christened 'Gnome Man's Land' by Harry, on account of the revolting, smirking gnome holding a blue fishing rod pointing in the direction of the dried-up pond. Mum's having a cigarette. She's asked me not to tell Dad about her return to 'the evil weed'. I'm learning a lot of things on Sunflower Ward – and not just about parents having secrets from each other.

I'm realising that watching telly all day is the most boring occupation on the planet and that playing battleships with Harry, who is a wizard strategist, is fast becoming the highlight of my day.

I know that keeping pain at bay is essential to not losing my sanity. I'm afraid of going to sleep in case I don't wake up again. And I'm starting to understand that counting the grapes in my fruit bowl can stop me being sucked into the dark, shadowy part of my mind, where something painful lays in wait for me, like a black monster in a pool, hoping to drown me in sorrow.

It has a name, this monster. It's called despair.

'When you're done here, can you pop over to bed eight, Sally?' asks Sister Beresford, poking her round, beaming face through a gap in the curtains. 'Little problem with the bedpan. Rupert's brother brought him some tadpoles, and guess where he thought he'd keep them?' She raises her eyes to the ceiling. 'I've told him they can stay in my office until he's well enough to put them in the hospital pond. Would you mind sorting it out?'

Nurse Emmerson grimaces at me. 'I hate frogs,' she says.

'Have you told her about Everest yet, Sally?' calls Harry, from behind the screen.

'Zip it, Higgins,' retorts Nurse Emmerson, a smile playing round her pink-lipsticked lips.

'It's hospital policy, called "Positive Thinking for Amputees", to tell you that some madman called Tom Whittaker climbed to the summit with a false right foot. And there was another one called Ashley Akers, who ran the London Marathon only a year after losing his leg in a land-mine explosion. So, Amy, how about you and me becoming the next legless free-fall parachute prodigies?'

'I'll think about it,' I reply.

'Could be...riveting.' Harry makes some unusual sounding frog noises.

'Ha, ha,' I say, unimpressed.

'Oh no,' I hear him groan, as a high-pitched voice shouts, 'Cooeey!' from the end of the ward. Several pairs of feet seem to be converging round his bed. There's the sound of kissing.

'Geroff, weirdos,' remonstrates Harry. 'What have you been eating, Sorcha? It stinks.'

'Pigerami,' replies a small voice.

'I've told you it's bad for you. Got all sorts of rubbish in it.'

'Sorry, Harry.'

'Hello, Poppikins, my darling,' says the breathy, high-pitched voice. And then the 'mwah, mwah' of two sloppy smackers being planted on unsuspecting cheeks.

'Mum, please...'

Nurse Emmerson grins at me as she winds a fresh dressing round my knee, which is like a swollen football.

'Poppikins?' I whisper, grateful to Harry's visitors for providing a distraction.

'Right. You're done,' says Nurse Emmerson, gently pulling back the white curtains. Five pairs of eyes greet me – including Harry's, looking exasperated. One of his three sisters has taken Ralph and put it on her head, back to front. I'm quite shocked to see that Harry has no hair, apart from a few fair wisps. But he does have a lipstick mark, right on top of his crown.

'Oooh, hello,' says his mum to me. 'You're new.'

'This is Amy, Mum,' says Harry, trying to discourage her from uttering anything embarrassing.

'Hello,' I smile at them all and reach for my headphones.

'Do you want some Pigerami?' asks one of the smaller girls, offering the chewed end of the protein stick. Harry's sisters, a pair of brown-haired twins of eight and a blonde girl of ten, are all sitting on his bed, chattering at him at once.

'Shut up, you little bludgers,' he says, firmly, and they do, their tanned faces full of respect and awe.

Mrs Higgins isn't at all what I expected. She looks like a model – with big blue eyes and wavy blonde hair. I notice that the male nurses are staring at her, probably because she is wearing a microskirt and high heels. She doesn't look much older than my sister, Caz.

'Harry, I've had this letter through from the tax people. I need you to look through it for me. Can't make head or tail of it and I've read it ten times…I told them on the phone my belly dancing was only casual not part-time…'

'I'll read it through later, Mum. Don't worry about it.'

'You're such a good boy, Harry,' coos his mother, fluttering her long lashes and giving him another kiss, on the forehead this time. 'Top of his class in all his subjects,' she says proudly. 'And here's me not even able to read a letter properly.'

'Mum's got dyslexiwotsit,' chirps one of the twins.

'I've got a silly brain which muddles things up. But Harry's always helped me – even when he was little. I keep telling him he's going to be prime minister one day.' She squeezes Harry's pale cheek affectionately. 'What would I do without you, Poppikins?'

Harry glances at me and raises his eyebrows. *Parents. What are they like?*

'All right, what's so funny?' asks Harry, as his family troops out of Sunflower Ward in search of ice creams.

'Nothing, Poppikins,' I smirk, not looking at him.

'It's a punishable offence, using that name in public.'

'I'm really scared,' I say, pretending to shake under my covers.

'It calls for retaliation of a vicious sort,' Harry warns.

'Well? I'm waiting.'

'You've asked for it. Lamey.'

'Pop Pop Poppikins.'

'Lamey Lamey Amy.'

'You didn't say you had sisters,' I remark, flicking nonchalantly through my magazine with the free lip balm stuck to the front.

Harry doesn't answer. When I look at him, he has his eyes closed and his hands clasped on his chest, as if he's dead.

'Very funny, Higgins.' I sigh. No response. 'You don't fool me.' Still no movement. 'I'm going to count to ten and then I'm calling Sister,' I warn. His left eye opens slowly and stares at me.

'It's F.O.S. It comes and goes…' he says, weakly.

Poor kid. He's got some other condition on top of everything else. Life is so unfair.

'What is it?' I ask.

'Family Overload Syndrome.' He smiles.

I throw my magazine at him. 'You're a pain. Your sisters are OK, though.' 'How would you know?'

'I've got one. Older than me. You'll meet her soon.'

Harry looks surprised. 'I thought you were an only.'

'Why?' I ask.

'The way your dad looks at you.'

'What do you mean?'

'When he's here in the morning.'

'What are you on about?' Harry isn't making any sense. Dad only comes in the evenings, after work, except at the weekend.

'Before you wake up. He sits and just looks at you. He's gone before breakfast.'

'You're making this up.' I'm getting cross now.

'Ask Sister,' he shrugs.

'I will,' I snap.

'Suit yourself.' And with that, Harry turns on his side away from me and pretends to go to sleep.

If Harry's right, why is Dad doing it? Why doesn't he come when I'm awake, with a bag of fresh chocolate croissants? Why would he just sit here? What's the point? Has he lost it? Does Mum know he comes? Should I ask her? So many questions. And no answers. Except one.

With every fibre of my body, I want it to be true.

9

Five thirty-five a.m. Everything's quiet on the ward, except for a strange whistling sound coming from Small Fry's nostrils four beds along from me. Sister Beresford is in her office, talking softly on the phone.

Morning light is filtering through the sunflower curtains, making the ward a warm yellow, like we're assorted sweets wrapped up in cellophane.

The rooks are up, caw-cawing noisily in the trees nearby. They are protecting their babies as they learn to spread their wings...

If they have a disabled baby, one who can't fly, what do they do? Do they still feed it and nurture it, or do they abandon it and let it starve, knowing it can never survive on its own in the wild?

He's still not here. I bet Harry was hallucinating.

I've been awake most of the night so that I don't miss him. It's like waiting for Santa. You want to hear the sleigh bells and the jingle of his hat. You wish so hard that your eyes nearly pop. But you daren't look, daren't see the magic at work, in case by witnessing it, you make it vanish.

It's five years since I believed in Father Christmas. Some kid with a shaved head called Sean told my whole class that the Santa thing was a whopper because he'd seen his dad making soot footprints by the fire, eating the mince pies and slurping the brandy. And when he cuddled the boy's mum and said 'Ho, ho, ho!' a pillow fell out of his red suit.

I'd already sussed it because we don't have a chimney and yet somehow, Santa managed to break through the double glazing every year without a sound and leave snowy footprints on the doormat, even when there was no snow. Caz tasted the white stuff and said it was like chalk. *Duh.* You want to humour them, your mum and dad. But sometimes they push their luck.

Five fifty a.m. Small Fry is smacking his lips now. Gross.

A light breeze is tickling the hair on my arms and causing a tiny shiver to run up my spine. When I look for its source, I see the curtains behind Harry's bed are puffed out at the bottom, like a Victorian crinoline. The outside air is stealing in under its skirts, invisible energy touching us as lightly as butterflies settling on flowers. Its freshness feels good after the heat of the night.

I try to count the goosebumps that have appeared on my arm. It's pointless and stupid but once my brain fixes on something, it has to see it through. It's an Amy thing. *Four hundred and ninety-two, four hundred and ninety-three...* I'm yawning and counting.

And now it's pitch black, but there is white light in the distance and the brightness illuminates a giant hopscotch grid on the ground. I'm standing on my good leg on the first square. Far ahead, maybe fifty metres away, I can see a figure jumping up and down, waving at me. I think it's a girl with long hair, but the light is so dazzling it's hard to see. There's something familiar about the waving, though – a kind of mad windmill action. My throat goes tight, just as I want to call out. I have to get closer, but that means hopping across the squares and how can I do that with only one leg...?

Sophie? Is that you? I can't come to you, even though I want to so much. Soph, can you hear me?

But now someone is taking my hand in theirs and leading me away from the grid. I'm looking back over my shoulder. The light is fading and so is the waving figure. Panic surges through my body.

'Wait!' I shout.

'Amy,' says a soft, deep voice. I open my eyes.

He's here.

I sit up and throw my arms round his neck, holding tight, as if onto a life raft in a raging sea.

'More dreams,' he says quietly, stroking my hair, which is damp against my cheeks. His calmness stills my pounding heart. Eventually, I let him go. He sits down on the chair next to my bed and takes my hand in his. He's wearing his work suit with a cream shirt. No tie. That will be in his pocket. He hasn't shaved yet either and looks a bit like George Clooney in *The Perfect Storm*.

There are bags under his eyes, big enough to put shopping in, as Mum would say. They make him look a bit bloodhoundy and cute.

'Harry said you've been coming in.' I smile.

'Yeah, well, you know what it's like at home in the morning. All I've got for company is Caz the Grump Monster and that New Age music compilation Mum uses for her salute to the sun.' He demonstrates with his arms up in homage. It makes me giggle.

'So coming here...?'

'Is light relief,' he affirms. He's still holding my hand, being careful to avoid the drip tube and needle.

'Not the best breakfast bar in town, though,' I suggest, wishing that sometimes, Dad would be honest with me.

'I often used to watch you sleeping when you were little,' he says at last, as if reading my thoughts. 'If I had a work problem and needed to sort it out in my head, seeing you breathing and dreaming and folding your tiny fingers up into your palms – somehow, it made sense of things. I imagined you growing before my eyes, like a magically engineered project, perfect...'

He's staring at the side of the bed now. I need him to tell me that it still makes sense of things, watching me. Even though I'm no longer perfect. But no words come. He simply squeezes my hand a little tighter.

When you find out the truth about Santa, something else more startling happens. You realise you're not a kid any more, but someone who knows that reindeer can't fly. So from now on, you're never going to look skyward, your heart vibrating in your ribs, hoping for a glimpse of sparkling sleigh dust. Somewhere deep in your soul, a door of possibility closes.

That's what this moment feels like. And we both sense it, Dad and I. The door hasn't just closed. It's slammed shut.

10

'Yours itching, Lamey?' Harry shouts.

I've got my headphones on, listening to the album chart.

'Mine are throbbing. Must be the heat…'

Yesterday, Harry didn't talk at all. Just threw up a lot. He says that happens, after the high dose of chemotherapy. He's having some every day this week – then he gets two weeks off to recover. I think they're worried about him, as Nurse Emmerson keeps taking his temperature and they've put him on a drip. He's as white as a ghost.

This morning, Caz told him he wouldn't have to dress up for Hallowe'en this year. 'That makes two of us then,' he replied, but I could tell he wasn't really full of his usual fighting spirit. He just muttered something about my sprocky sister. 'Sprocky', in Harry-speak, is the opposite of 'spangly'.

'What's Number One, then?' he asks, with his eyes closed.

'Dunno. The Vomit Monkeys are number six,' I reply.

'Do you think they'd let me audition? I'd be a natural,' he sighs.

'They could learn a thing or two from you, Poppikins.' I grin at him.

'Thanks,' he says, opening one eye and staring at me. 'I think I qualify as a professional by now. How're you doing today, Lamey?'

I don't have time to answer. Mum is brandishing a wheelchair at the end of the bed. Nurse Emmerson's coming to lend a hand. It's a right palaver with the drip needle in my hand. That has to be disconnected first and now I feel a bit faint. And very wobbly. I want to put my right foot down to balance me. But that, of course, is impossible.

'See ya later,' calls Harry quietly, as Mum wheels me away.

I can tell she doesn't approve of him very much. She thinks he's a bad influence – after Sister Beresford mentioned our elastic-band-pinging competition that caused Nurse Emmerson to drop a whole tray of urine samples. I don't care. Harry and I are soulmates. We've even got birthdays within a few days of each other. Although he's an Aries (fiery ram) and I'm a Taurus (stubborn bull). He says that's a 'disaster, astrologically speaking'.

We follow signs to the Prosthetics Department, a five-minute push away from the ward – where a smiley, plump woman called Pam tells me I am expected. Prostheses are false body parts, and Mum pushes me past a glass-fronted room where people are busy making them on workbenches. It looks like Santa's grotto, except the presents they are crafting so carefully aren't pretty dolls and teddies but assorted arms, legs, hands and feet.

'How do you feel about walking today, Amy?' asks a short guy with masses of untidy blond hair. 'I'm Ed, by the way. Your very own prosthetist. I'll be making your new leg.' He looks intently at my stump, measures it with a tape and writes down the numbers on his clipboard notepad. 'I can fix you up with a temporary one today, so you can be away with your crutches and dump the chair. Sound good?'

It's too much information. I've only just got out of bed. Stupid tears start welling up in my eyes. I look at Mum in panic – Mum instinctively reaches into her bag for the Fox's Glacier Mints, her answer to everything – arguments, injuries, shock, joy, boredom and nuclear holocaust.

'Mint, anyone?' she asks, stuffing an unwrapped one straight in my mouth. Magically, the menthol makes my stinging tears subside.

'I'm diabetic. Have to keep off the sweets,' says Ed, 'although I have a bag of lemon sherbets for special occasions. But that's our secret. Don't tell my girlfriend or she'll steal them.'

I look at him in a new light. What could be worse than a life based on sweet rationing?

Ed disappears into Santa's grotto and returns with half a leg under his arm. It looks silly. I can't help laughing. Mum is sucking extra hard on her mint as Ed shows me how to do the straps up round my knee to hold the leg on. My fingers are fumbling with the buckle.

'Deep breath,' says Ed, taking my hands and helping me up out of the chair.

I stand, trying not to put weight on my new leg. It feels really strange. He gives me a pair of crutches and asks me to take a few steps. The first one sends pain searing up my stump and into my spine.

'That's really great, Amy,' he encourages.

Mum is pretending to blow her nose. I can tell she's crying.

'It hurts,' I say, dismally.

'Your new leg will fit much more comfortably,' Ed reassures me. 'After a while, you won't even know it's there.'

Some hope. The realisation that I am always going to walk like a circus performer brings me to a complete standstill.

'I can't do it,' I say, quietly, my head cast down to the floor. My shoulders are heaving involuntarily and tears are cascading down my cheeks. Mum is at my side, supporting me, just as my legs buckle and give way. Ed helps me back into the wheelchair and holds my hands.

'That was a fantastic start,' he insists. 'Every day, you'll get stronger, with practice. Once all the swelling has gone, I'll be able to take a plaster cast and start moulding your new leg...'

With my crutches across my lap, Mum wheels me out past the grotto, through the reception area and back into the long corridor that smells of disinfectant. We are both silent, lost in our own thoughts.

Are you there, Sophie? Can you see what I've become?

Brain to Amy, brain to Amy. Message alert. You are not who you were. You are half a leg short of a pair and are now a cripple (can't say that, not politically correct) or rather, an official disabled person who can forget about gold medals at the Olympics, unless you train for the hopping race, but not sure that is recognised yet as an Olympic sport. As for swimming, well, you'd be all right if the pool were round, as you can only go in circles. Terrible end to a promising career, but that's the way the cookie crumbles. Just one more thing: amputees often feel pain in the bit that's been chopped or blown off. It doesn't mean you are going mad, just that brains have trouble coping with body parts that go missing. Over and out.

11

We're all here, all the kids from Sunflower Ward, apart from the Indian girl who arrived late last night after swallowing a golf ball. It's a 'very special day', according to Sister Beresford. It's the day she finally gets rid of 'those flipping frogs' from her office. Rupert is about to release them into the newly renovated pond in the hospital garden. As tadpoles, they have already experienced life in a water-filled bedpan, followed by an incubator. There must be about seventy of them, like tiny black marbles, with legs.

'Gently does it, Rupert,' encourages Sister Beresford as he starts to tip the cascading frogs over the new lilies into the pond. His grin is so broad it seems to rest on his neck brace. He looks like the Cheshire Cat from *Alice in Wonderland*. His older brother, Mark, is taking digital photos, mostly of the frogs.

'Wicked!' Rupert declares, shaking the last creature from its glass sanctuary with a 'plop'.

I've seen this before, in my dreams. I'm one of the frogs, hitting the surface of the water for the first time, descending into the darkness, seeing the light recede. It feels very cold and when I try to push out with my legs, nothing happens…

'Amy, you OK?' asks Harry, who is sharing a small wooden seat with me. He has green icing on his lips from the frog cake Rupert's Mum brought us for the occasion.

'Yeah,' I reply. 'Just a bit weird.'

''Course you are.' He grins.

'Do them turn into princes?' asks Jasmine, Rupert's little sister, who is four and has curly red hair. She has a captive frog in her hand and is trying to lick it with her tongue.

'Only in films, dear,' sighs Sister Beresford. 'Back to the ward now, everyone.'

And with a clap of her hands, Sister ushers the small crowd of kids, nurses and a few parents out of Gnome Man's Land. She winks at Harry and me as she passes and suddenly, we are left alone.

'Sprocky cake.' He grimaces, wiping his mouth. 'Lucky you avoided it.'

'Don't eat cake when I'm—' I stop short and realise what I'm about to say. My training regime hardly ever allows sweet treats – and things with icing are banned by Mum on tooth-decay grounds, except on birthdays. I feel a shiver pass down my spine and with it, the realisation that I will never be officially 'in training' as a county swimmer again. I have a lump in my throat, and my eyes start to sting with tears.

Harry notices this. 'Very overrated thing, sponge,' he says, throwing his last lumps of icing at Boris the gnome. 'Biscuits are something else. In terms of things you most crave, they are up there with that girl in *My Sister the Sumo Wrestler*. Hard to decide a top three, but I think it would have to be fig rolls, jammy dodgers and—'

'Harry,' I interject, staring at him with narrowed eyes.

'Yup?' he says, innocently.

'Don't.' Don't try to make me feel better, because you can't.

We sit in silence. There's an occasional 'plip, plop' as a froglet flips into the pond. A bird is singing somewhere nearby. I feel quite angry that it's so cheerful. I wish I had a catapult. Harry is watching me out of the corner of his eye.

'You'll be out of here soon, Lamey,' he states, without turning his head towards me.

'Yeah, right,' I reply, sarcastically. They're hardly going to discharge a girl who can't manage even a few stupid steps on her temporary leg.

'Don't suppose you'll miss me,' he says, checking his fingernails.

'Like a boil on my bum, probably,' I retort, instantly regretting it. Honestly, I open my mouth these days and really rude stuff comes out.

'Not very nice, is it, Boris?' says Harry to the gnome, who is facing us and smirking more than usual.

'She must be banished from this sacred space and sent to the grotto for reconfiguring,' replies a squeaky voice, which I am supposed to believe comes from Boris.

'Zip it,' I warn, shaking my crutch at the faded fiend.

'Don't be cruel,' says Harry. 'He has a heart.'

'Oh, really?' I scoff.

'Yes, but it was accidentally turned to clay when he was part of the Human Gen-gnome Project.'

'You're such a smart arse,' I say. 'You're the only one who reads those ancient medical magazines in the day room.'

'Better than being a dumbarse.' Harry smiles, smugly.

Silence again. We both have our arms crossed. Mum says this is a defensive thing that people do when they want to shield themselves from a difficult situation. What am I defending myself against here? Harry's amazing wit – not?

I'm staring at my temporary leg, which is sticking out of my jogging bottoms. Harry's eyes drift downwards to follow my gaze.

'I used to dream of looking like her when I was little,' I confess.

'Who?' he asks.

'Barbie.'

'Quite pink, isn't it?' he observes. 'Should be careful what you wish for. I asked for pins like 007 and look what happened to me.' He points to his slim, pyjama-ed legs stretched out straight in front of him. 'Got a pair from the Royal Ballet.'

I'm aware that my breathing is very tight, all of a sudden. That only happens when I'm worried about something, or standing on the springboard, my team watching me, waiting to dive...

'You worried about something?' asks Harry, taking my hand and giving it a squeeze. God, he must be a mind-reader. His gentle grip feels light and cool and reassuring. It's the first time we've touched. His fingers rest next to mine for a moment – and then they're gone. It's like being brushed by butterfly wings...

'Got to walk the plank tomorrow,' I tell him. This is amputee-speak for standing on the moving treadmill in the Gait-Analysis Department, where they measure how much pressure you're putting on your stump. I haven't even thought about it until now, though, so that can't be the real reason why I'm uptight.

'You'll have wires all over your legs like spaghetti,' demonstrates Harry. 'Don't ask them to explain the graph at the end because they go into geek-speak and it's dead boring. The great thing is, Ed'll use the info to build your new leg. So it's brilliant. Now show me the clown and cheer me up.'

'The clown?'

'Well, you're not going to walk like a supermodel to start with, are you?' He raises his eyebrows at me.

I'm getting better with the crutches, but my Barbie leg is rubbing on my stump with each step. It makes my eyes water. My arms get really sore helping to support my weight, and my wrists ache where my hands grip the grey handles. But, hey. Ed says I'll be able to walk without the crutches with practice.

Yeah, and frogs might fly…

Harry is watching me intently as I make a slow circuit of the pond, trying not to squash small hoppers. I can feel myself flushing.

'Faster!' shouts my tormentor as I shuffle past. 'You know I've got a low boredom threshold,' he groans. 'Whassat, Boris?' he asks, leaning towards the gnome. 'Boris says you're total rubbish.'

'Shut your face.' There I go again. Mum thinks I'm getting hormonal, which accounts for me being quite 'snappy' and 'mouthy' at the moment. She is sure this is partly due to Harry initiating me into teenage tantrums and partly due to missing the stimulus of school. To remedy this, she has been bringing me some maths and English homework from my teacher, Miss Gates. The latest essay title is 'My Perfect Future'.

I have trouble thinking beyond tomorrow.

Sweat beads are forming on my forehead. My arms feel shaky now. A wave of nausea flows up from my stomach to my throat.

'Harry, I…' My eyes are looking down dark tunnels and I'm wobbling. I think I'm going to faint, but Harry is suddenly at my side, holding me by my elbows. I haven't noticed before that he's taller than me.

'Two steps back to the seat,' he says gently, putting his arms round me. 'I've got you. You won't fall.'

'I'm stuck,' I tell him. My right leg isn't responding at all. My stump feels like it's burning. My brain has gone into free fall.

'Just hop on your left leg, then,' Harry says encouragingly.

I do this and he helps me ease down onto the seat. My heart is pounding, and my nose is running with the exertion of the walking. Great! I've only got my sweatshirt sleeve to wipe it on. I shake my head, full of self-pity. Harry is bending down, looking into my face, very concerned.

'No one can do this straight away,' he says. 'Not even Amy "the Champ" Curtis.'

Plip, plop. A frog dives into the pond. Another jumps onto Harry's right foot. He hasn't noticed. My mouth curls into a grin.

'What?' he asks, suspicious.

'Passenger,' I reply, pointing down.

'Oi, geroff, you,' he says, promptly jerking his leg upwards and sending the green amphibian into the air. 'Witness the new genus of *Hopus aeronauticus*.'

I give him a quizzical look, waiting to be impressed.

'That's flying frog, to you.' He grins.

12

Caz, Harry and I are playing cheat in the Day Room. I've left my temporary leg off for a bit after this morning's frog fiesta. I'm back in my dressing gown, which is lying flat and forlorn against the chair where my right leg should be.

Small Fry is watching kids' telly – a cartoon featuring characters with square heads. He keeps sniffing and laughing at the same time. Sometimes, he laughs so much, his voice disappears completely and he just wheezes.

Caz is struggling to stay in the game. We keep catching her out and she gets all uppity and asks us how we know she's lying.

'You wrinkle your nose each time you tell porkies,' observes Harry.

'I don't,' she says, defensively, doing it. 'Anyway, since when did you become an expert in body language?'

'Read everything in the mobile library from A to P so far,' he says, 'including two books on lie detection techniques used by the CIA.'

'You're making that up,' says Caz, narrowing her eyes at him.

Harry just shrugs, smugly.

'OK… Four queens,' I smile, laying the cards down emphatically.

Harry gives me a shrewd look.

'But they can't be,' says Caz. 'You put two queens down last time, so *cheat*.'

I turn the cards over, revealing four queens. Caz gives me a glare and scoops the huge pile from the centre of the coffee table onto her already tall mound. Her lip is protruding slightly, which is her normal reaction when I beat her at games.

'You have to have a strategy,' I tell her.

'It's just a card game,' she replies, huffily. 'And actually I'm quite bored.'

'A-ha, a-hahahahaha,' laughs Small Fry, clutching his stomach. Snot falls from his nose onto the carpet. We all groan in disgust.

'Sthorry.' He grins.

'I'm out of here,' says Caz.

'Remember the deal?' asks Harry.

'Yeah, yeah. Loser buys the ice creams.' Poor Caz. She's a regular at the corner shop near the hospital now, usually with a list from Harry and me. We've beaten her at hangman, Scrabble and cheat this week. There is always a penalty for losing. She has to grant our wishes. Our very own personal slave.

Harry and I really get into the competitive thing. We play the best of three and it's always closely fought. We spent four hours playing draughts yesterday. I had a headache after concentrating so hard. I won by setting a trap with my kings. Harry had no way out. We shook hands afterwards. I could tell he was quite impressed. Last night I caught him analysing my strategy on paper.

'Just admit you were beaten by a genius, loser,' I smirked.

'Sussed you.' He grinned, folding the paper into an aeroplane and launching it at me. 'You're finished.'

He doesn't let me get away with anything. Not even feeling sorry for myself. If I'm mopey, he tells me to 'put my best foot forward'. Usually he has the last word too, but at lunchtime today we were arguing about the best way to poach an egg (the strange, rubbery, white thing inside the pork pie inspired this conversation) and I told him to back down because, as someone who has only ever used a microwave to make instant porridge, he didn't have a leg to stand on.

Ha!

'Fancy another game of hangman?' asks Harry.

'Think I've killed you enough times today, Poppikins,' I yawn, stretching my arms up into the warm summer-evening air above my head.

'Three games all, actually,' he corrects me, twizzling a pencil between his thumb and index finger.

'Nah. Going to the loo,' I say, putting my arms through the semi-circular grips at the top of my crutches. I let my left leg take the strain and push up. It feels so strange without its partner. I close my eyes for a moment and hope with every fibre of my body that when I open them again, my right leg will be there and I'll be on the crossing with Sophie and we'll be safely stepping up onto the kerb as the lorry goes past...

I wonder if the driver has gone to court yet. I've asked Dad about it, but he said I shouldn't think about that at the moment. I try not to. It makes me start shaking. Then Harry has to give me chocolate to calm me down and he says it's costing him a fortune because the sweets sold by the volunteers from the mobile trolley are thirty per cent more expensive than the corner shop.

My eyelids start to lift slowly, and instead of revealing Small Fry and Harry and the indisputable truth of my situation, there is something large and familiar and fantastic filling my gaze.

'Dan!' I shriek and lift my arms up, almost falling towards him as he scoops me up in a great big hug. He's holding flowers in one hand. I can smell their heavy fragrance.

'Hello, champ,' he says, lifting me off the ground and then putting me back down gently.

'Your mum said you were ready for a visit. So here I am.'

'They for me?' I ask, indicating the exotic pink and white blooms.

'Stargazer lilies. For our star.' He smiles, presenting them to me. He's wearing our team shirt, as always, dark-blue jogging bottoms and a white baseball cap. Mum told me he's been away with my team in France – one of the mini-Euro galas which happen each summer. It must have been very hot there. His face is much browner than the last time I saw him. I want to hear all about it but something is moving strangely inside me, some dark thing with a cold, green stare and a heart of stone...

'Dan, this is Harry. He bullies me about everything, just like you,' I say. Harry pulls a face of mock outrage and they shake hands.

'Giving you a hard time, this one, is she?' Dan asks.

'Twenty-four seven,' he replies. 'I'm hoping my next neighbour is mute.'

'Ha, hahahahahah,' laughs Small Fry, on his belly on the floor, eyes fixed on the screen as if hypnotised.

'Let's go to the ward, Dan,' I suggest, suddenly feeling claustrophobic in this room as memories and emotions course through my brain. The last time I saw this guy, I was his top athlete. I'm realising two things as I look at his warm smile. Our relationship has changed for ever. And he's not my coach any more.

He walks with me slowly along the corridor leading back to Sunflower Ward, chatting about the team and who's doing what, observing the massive effort I need to use the crutches and my one leg to move me forward. I wish I hadn't taken my temporary leg off now. At least with that on, I look half way normal.

I'm so happy to see Dan. And so embarrassed I could cry. He waits for me while I go to the loo – which for me involves about five minutes of awkward manoeuvring just to have a pee and wash my hands. He's leaning against the wall when I emerge, my flowers held at his side, and some of the colour seems to have drained from his face. Maybe it's just a trick of the light and the evening shadows.

'Sorry,' I apologise.

'I wasn't timing you,' he grins.

No, Dan, you won't ever be timing me again.

'So, young lady, I have some good news, which I thought you might like to hear.' This is always how he tells me that my personal-best times have improved by a certain percentage, enabling us to introduce a new training schedule that is even more challenging than the last. But that's not a possibility now.

I know what he's going to say. I can see long tables covered in white cloths, plates and glasses and all my team and their parents in smart gear…

'We'd like to invite you to be our guest of honour at the team dinner next month, Amy. You don't have to make up your mind now. Just think about it.'

I stop mid-hop, and just look at the floor, taking this in. I've gone from being a team member to just a guest in a nanosecond. It's like Dan has suddenly cut the cord securing me to the thing that has given me life for so long. Now I'm an outsider and there's no way back.

'Right,' I manage.

'Hope you'll come and see us before that, of course,' he adds, giving my shoulders a squeeze. 'In fact, I'd like to talk to you about helping me with coaching. Later on. What do you think?'

I open my mouth but no words come. In my head, I hear the terrible cry of a lost child, cast out against its will, alone in a wilderness. I'm aware that I'm rocking a little. My vision feels blurred. I want to curl up and go to sleep.

'Wake up, idiot. A step at a time!' Sophie's voice is in my head.

Don't you start nagging me, Soph. That's all I need ...

'Would you like me to get your chair?' asks Dan, concerned.

'No,' I reply, with renewed determination. 'I'll get there.'

'That's my girl,' he says.

13

'Hello, Amy – sorry about the time. There was nowhere to park. Some procession in the street… People on stilts,' Mum pants, in a flap. She looks quite flustered.

It's the annual march to publicise the circus. That means this is my eighth week in hospital, in my safe cocoon, protected from the outside world and its dangers and opportunities. I do get bulletins from the real world, from my mates in the swimming team, who keep appearing with suntans and stories of their holidays in Devon and Tenerife and Disney World and the chocolate factory in Switzerland. Dan pops in once a week with the gossip from training sessions – he's really hoping I'll go for this coaching thing, and has left me some leaflets about the qualifications I'd need to aim for. Even our neighbour Joan has come twice. Each time she has brought a paper bag full of strange fruit and whispered in my ear that the grapes were on 'special' and I should leave the brown ones…

Shirley and Gus still haven't come. Not even once. They sent a card with a retriever on it a while ago. Inside, Gus drew a guinea pig with a speech bubble saying, 'mis you'.

Mum is looking around for a spare wheelchair.

''s'OK Mum, I'll walk,' I say lightly.

'Are you sure that's a good…' she stops herself and just nods.

'See you, Poppikins.' I smile at Harry, who raises a hand but doesn't look up from the book – *The Paranormal* – his mum brought him from the library.

On the way down to the grotto, I mention to Mum that I haven't seen Dad at all this week.

'He's still working on that design job in Leeds,' she replies, rather too quickly. 'I'm sure he'll phone when he gets a minute.'

Mum and Dad don't seem to be getting on too well these days.

I remember that even when he went to Dubai on contract for three months as part of a team of architects creating the world's first seven-star hotel, he managed to call home every day.

'Sometimes men like to go into man-caves,' says Mum. I'm not sure what she means by this. Are there caves in Leeds? And are they full of men in suits?

Downstairs, Carla the physiotherapist, who is a Goth and wears four spiky earrings in each ear plus studs in her eyebrow and tongue, hooks my real and unreal legs up to several monitors with wires like spaghetti and asks me to step onto the walking machine, using the grab bars at the side to balance. 'I'm going to turn the machine on,' she explains in a Brummie accent, 'and I'd like you to start walking normally, Amy. Can you do that for me?'

Duh?

Suddenly, the black walkway starts to move backwards very slowly and even though I begin to put one foot in front of the other, I can't keep up with it and find myself hopping on my left leg and holding on tight with my arms. 'Focus on your pace – breathe – get into a rhythm…' Dan's relentless training echoes in my mind. But this isn't the 200-metre freestyle. It is Everest and the summit seems a lifetime away.

Second attempt, and miraculously, my legs are behaving now. Thanks, Dan – you're still my hero. The floor is moving and I'm walking with even strides.

'Let go of the bars, Amy. You're doing really well,' says Carla, engrossed in the lines zigzagging across her computer screens.

Beads of sweat are forming on my brow with the effort of the pace. My Barbie leg is rubbing more with each step. I don't think I can keep this up much l/nger. I close my eyes and imagine I am in the pool and the finish line is fifty metres away. I can hear the vibration of the crowd through my body, my heart is banging in my chest, and…

'OK, that's fine,' says Carla, slowing the machine.

I grab the bars on either side. My arms and my legs are shaking. It's difficult to step down. Mum is ready with my crutches.

'I'll explain the data when you've seen Ed,' says the tattooed moth on Carla's back. I think I am hallucinating.

There are two Eds. They are both speaking at once. 'Did you hear me, Amy?' repeats one of them. As I stare at them, they morph into one familiar face, which is smiling at me. 'I said, today's a special day.'

'International Women's Day in Latvia?' I mutter, remembering that Harry has imparted this dazzling fact to me after reading the back of the *Times Educational Supplement*, which is all he could find to annoy me with in the Day Room.

'You can pack your things. You're coming home tomorrow, Amy,' says Mum, eyes full of mist.

Home. Back to a life that isn't any more. No more Sunflower Ward. No more Harry.

'You'll be popping back to see me once a week,' says Ed, cheerfully. 'Your new leg will be ready in a fortnight, and after that we'll be adjusting it and helping your muscles with more physio.'

My chin is on my chest. I am crying silently.

'It's relief, I expect,' says Mum, slightly hurt, stroking my arm.

14

'On your marks!' says Caz, holding up the latest copy of *Babes* magazine in the air.

'Whose stupid idea was this?' I ask, my hands hovering over the tyres of my wheelchair.

'Yours, Lamey,' says Harry, a few inches away from me in his chair, facing down the corridor.

'Get set!' shouts my sister, milking it.

'I'm worried that you're going to take defeat very badly,' says Harry.

'If you want to back out, you only have to say,' I reply.

'GO!'

Harry has named this race the 'Clash of the Up-Titans'. It's my last morning in hospital, so our final chance to decide the ultimate victor or victrix. We've added up our cumulative scores for the various games we have played throughout the last two months – and we have 3,000 points each.

Quite a coincidence.

So, the first one of us to pass through the heavy plastic flap partition wins. We've chosen this corridor because it's one of the longest in the hospital and it leads to the Department of Tropical Diseases. There are rumours that the patients all have illnesses with horrible names like dengue fever and anthrax and they're manacled to their beds and not allowed to wander about.

'Humiliation is just seconds away, Lamey,' says Harry, as he attempts to add turbo power to his wheel-spinning. He is leaning forward, pathetically trying to make himself more aerodynamic.

We are neck and neck...

'Watch and learn,' I reply as adrenaline pumps through my system and my once strong arms at last find their rhythm. We are only four spins away from the partition and I'm surging past my adversary.

But now Harry's right here with me. Flip a frog, how did he manage that? He's too close and our wheels are locking together, like in Roman chariot contests. And now a trolley with a long, unmoving thing covered in a sheet is being pushed through the partition and someone with a deep voice is shouting at us but we're not going to be able to stop in time...

'You little shysters – no respect for the dead,' mutters the hospital porter, helping to lift Harry, who is sprawled on the floor with his head under the trolley. 'You can't go tearing about the corridors, terrorising everybody. Now clear off, the pair of yer.'

We wait a moment while the disgruntled man pushes the squeaking trolley down the corridor, from where Caz has mysteriously disappeared. Then Harry holds out his hand.

'Officially a tie, then,' he says.

'Saved by a stiff, more like,' I reply.

'I see we'll have to settle this some other time, Lamey.'

'Obviously,' I reply, very cool, even though my whole body is hot from exertion.

Harry and I exchange serious glances and suddenly we are laughing – laughing so hard our stomachs are going into spasm and our ribs are aching and tears are pouring down our cheeks. I've never seen Harry cry and for some reason this makes me convulse even more. Every time we try to stop and calm down and breathe, one of us starts up again. Harry manages to utter 'trolley', and I am almost on the floor, rolling around. Never in my life have I found anything more funny than this moment. I wish I could press the 'Save' button…

15

It's my last hour here. I've been sitting with Mum in Gnome Man's Land. She's having another sneaky cigarette while Dad is finding a parking space.

She's probably a smokeaholic by now.

She said she and Dad are having 'problems' but it wasn't anything to worry about. And these 'problems' weren't my fault, or Caz's, they were just things that happen between parents sometimes.

I never thought they would happen to mine. Now I've got to worry about them AND say goodbye to Harry...

Yellow afternoon light is shafting through the long row of windows in the corridor leading to Sunflower Ward, which, in a matter of minutes, will be just a weird dream, one in which all the kids are aliens.

In here, we're all bound by a common experience – sickness or injury. Many of us have stood at the edge of the precipice. We've stared into the darkness at death and looked away. The reasons that have brought us here have also stolen our childhood. We look at life through eyes which have seen too much. Eyes that belong to kids who are now time-travellers.

I stop for a moment and let the warmth envelop me. Golden sun wraps itself round my body like silk.

My nerves tingle with the sensation of its touch. The corridor is luminous, its grey polished floor a translucent sea. And in the distance, dancing in a pool of sun, is a child in a white robe with angel-blonde hair.

'Sophie!' I call out.

The child stops dancing and looks at me shyly. Her face is unfamiliar. She puts her fingers to her lips and whispers, 'Shhhh,' before waving and running away, back to the place she has escaped from.

'You look like you've seen a ghost,' says Harry, as I swing my legs up onto my bed and lie back on my pillows, exhausted. I just close my eyes and try to settle the thousand thoughts which are tumbling through my brain.

'Would you like my magnetic battleships game?' I ask him.

'No one to play it with,' he says, matter-of-factly. 'This lot are all too thick. They have a combined IQ of a pint of custard.' This is meant to be a compliment. 'I've made something for you,' he says, rummaging around in his drawer and producing a handmade envelope, held together with surgical tape. 'Sorry. About the tape.' He shrugs.

Inside is a card with a pencil cartoon, depicting me wobbling about on crutches and Harry in a sports car and the words 'Lean on Me' across the top.

'"To Lamey, from your mate Harry. Hop it,"' I read aloud. There's another cartoon of a plastic pink leg doing just that, in the corner, and a scribbled address and

Hotmail contact. 'Cool. Thanks.'

'Lamey?'

'Yes, Poppikins?'

'Don't suppose you'll come and visit me?'

'Probably not.'

'Good decision. The best. The next person in your bed is bound to be better-looking. I'll soon forget you.'

I smile at him. He grins back at me, white-faced and dark-eyed under Ralph, the racoon hat. Then he pulls a face. I follow his gaze as it moves from me to a purple pipe cleaner, approaching.

'God, it's so hot in here. I can't bear it,' says my sister loudly, sitting heavily on my bed and helping herself to my grapes.

Caz has apparently returned to help me pack my things. She is showing acres of flat stomach above her skin-tight purple trousers. She is also wearing a new maroon lipstick and pink eye shadow, bought during the retail therapy that followed our 'totally embarrassing' incident on the second floor.

'I got you a present.' She beams, thrusting a carrier bag onto my lap. Inside is a pink microtop with 'Babe' spelled out in silver studs, a bit like the one in Caz's navel. 'It was in the sale. I looked at it and thought of you…'

Was that because most of it is missing? I smile and say 'thanks'. Caz is still grinning very strangely.

'Aren't you going to ask me?' she implores.

'Ask you what?'

'Why I'm so happy.'

'Why are you so happy?'

'Marcus Boddington's asked me out.'

I glance at Harry. He is feigning unconsciousness. His mouth is open, paralysed with boredom. I grin at my sister.

'Great, Caz,' I say, managing to sound like I mean it.

'Isn't it?' she breathes, biting into a grape. 'He wrote me this poem – do you want to hear it?'

Harry starts to make gurgling and choking noises, as if he's going to throw up.

'That's so gross,' whispers Caz. 'How do you put up with that?'

'It's hard, especially when he vomits blood and swallows his tongue,' I say, seriously.

'I'll show it to you later. Actually, I think I need some fresh air. I'll go and find Mum.'

And she's gone. Harry turns to me and pulls a face. 'She's even sprockier than before,' he says.

'Tell me about it,' I groan.

And now there's an awkward silence between us. For two kids who've hardly stopped talking for weeks, it's weird. And then I notice Harry is wearing jeans and a sweatshirt, plus Ralph.

'Going somewhere, then?' I ask.

'Thought you might like a lift in my chariot,' he says, indicating his wheelchair. 'Not exactly a Porsche, but you'll have to be patient.'

'Wish you were going home too, Poppikins,' I manage to say at last.

'Food's better here.' He grins. 'And I don't have to watch Mum practising her belly-dancing...' He has a strangely serene smile on his face, which he only ever puts on to annoy me.

'What?' I ask.

'Just thinking, won't have to put up with any more of your snoring...'

I throw my pillow at him just as Mum appears with Caz, and suddenly everything happens in a whirl. She's packing my fruit, all the get-well cards and my photo of Barker. Caz puts my games and clothes in a plastic laundry box, her lip slightly raised every time she has to go near Harry.

Everyone's waving goodbye. Isabella gives me a kiss on both cheeks and says something husky in Spanish. The new boy, who moved into Small Fry's bed the day he went home with his foster family, is waggling his head about to music coming via his iPod to his earpiece.

Sister Beresford is smiling. 'Have a lovely trip home.' She waves as we move past her in procession. I take a last look round Sunflower Ward.

'Good luck, you guys. I'll come and see you all,' I tell them, knowing that by the time of my next appointment, many of them will have gone home to face their lives in the real world again.

'Dad's waiting on double yellows,' says Mum, urging me on.

'Right then,' says Harry, motioning for me to sit on his lap in the wheelchair.

I pass my crutches to Mum and ease myself down on Harry, hoping I won't crush him to bits. I put my arms round his neck. My cheeks are flushing hot with the sudden contact.

'God, you weigh a ton.' He cringes, and we set off at about fifteen miles per hour out of the ward.

We have to dodge the same porter from this morning pushing a frail old man on a trolley. 'Oi!' he shouts, as we pass. 'What did I tell you two little shysters?' Everyone else in the corridor stands to the side as a precaution. I can almost feel the wind in my hair again.

Mum and Caz catch us up in reception. Mum gives me my crutches and manages to smile at Harry.

'Thanks, Poppikins,' I say, and without thinking give him a kiss on the cheek.

'Geroff, weirdo,' he protests, wiping it away.

'Bye then,' I manage, although it's hard to smile because my bottom lip is starting to tremble.

'Be cool, Lamey. See you around.' And with that, he spins the chair round and zooms away, waving Ralph, the racoon hat, in the air and yelling, 'Hi ho Silver…'

Harry Higgins. Living legend.

16

So, after rolling round with an ecstatic Barker on the hall floor and going upstairs backwards on my bum, I'm here in my own room, where everything is as I left it two months ago. Actually, that's not quite true. It's tidy, for a start. Mum's been in like a whirling dervish with the Hoover and a duster and it looks like a feature in one of those glossy home-makeover magazines, complete with a vase of flowers. 'This is Amy's bedroom, where pink and orange create a vibrant contrast of mood, enhanced by a green inflatable armchair and a fashionably stained but cute Dalmatians scatter rug...'

It's like I'm in a museum. My swimming medals still line my walls. My chicken clock is still ticking. The only thing that is different is me. I'm not the same Amy who left this room all those weeks ago, jumped downstairs two at a time and left the house with my best friend. I'm minus twenty-five per cent of my walking apparatus. I feel like an impostor – like these things don't belong to me any more...

Five minutes later and I'm lying on my bed eating chunky-chip cookies and Dad is rabbiting on about researchers in the UK who are working on the growth of new body parts, using stem cells. I nod and say, 'Coolio,' but I'm not taking it in. I'm feeling spaced out and guilty that I'm not overwhelmed by how great it is to be in my room with all my things round me. I don't feel connected with my possessions any more. They are part of a life that has passed.

I need to be on my own for a while, Dad, don't you understand?

My eyes rest on the pink-and-orange helium balloon at the end of my bed, which says, 'You're a Star' – a present from Caz. It's a bit strange to get balloons when your life feels like it's lost its buoyancy.

When Dad goes to get me a lemonade, I take Sophie's silver teddy out of my jeans pocket and stare at it, reminding myself that this is really all that remains of our friendship. I notice that the photos of the two of us have been removed from the top of my bookcase, but that's OK. Mum knows the images would be too much for me today. I'm wondering why Shirley and Gus haven't been in touch… Maybe we can ask them over for tea now I'm back. It would be so great to see them.

So far, returning home has been as low key as Mum and Dad can make it – no surprise parties or mates jumping out from behind the sofa. Dad helps me downstairs, and Mum gives me two bouquets – one from Dan and the swimming team and one from my school. There's even some lucky heather from Joan next door. She's tied the stems together with an old shoelace.

Life may be sort of normal, but we are all different.

Even Barker is having to get used to a new bed, having chewed up his old one in protest at being left alone during my family's hospital visits. He looks white-eyed and miserable in his new plastic doghouse, despite the treat of a yellow plastic squeaky toy bone.

I give him a big hug. 'It's not that bad,' I whisper to him. He wags his tail.

Dad kisses my forehead and tweaks my nose, just like he used to. 'It's great to have you home, kiddo,' he says. 'And in honour of a special occasion, I'm going to cook tonight.'

Caz and I both groan.

'No, it'll be fine. We're having burritos and Mum's made the filling. I'm just arranging the tortillas and – well – grating the cheese.'

'No mystery ingredients,' I plead. Normally, he adds any old thing he finds in the fridge, thinking that the more flavours there are, the better. I've told him that cauliflower isn't a natural thing to have with bolognese sauce, but he doesn't listen.

So, after watching two of my favourite DVDs, curled up with Mum and Caz on the sofa, the afternoon has passed and darkness is spreading across the sky, like a curtain being drawn across the first act of my new life. I'm wondering what Harry is doing and whether there's another kid in my hospital bed now. It feels strange not having him around.

Mum lights candles and Caz lays the table. Everyone

bustles round me, making things happen. I'm even more spaced out now. Probably suffering from F.O.S. I'm used to having time on my own. Now I'm part of a unit again.

Dinner is great – especially after weeks of hospital food. I can't eat that much, as my stomach has shrunk, but I manage a whole burrito with soured cream on top and nachos on the side. Mum makes us drink a toast to health and happiness and I'm allowed some wine for the first time.

After some homemade strawberry ice cream, Mum and Dad say it's a good time to tell us something. They look a bit apprehensive, so it's not something excellent, like a holiday on a palm-fringed beach. Caz and I exchange glances. I hope they're not getting divorced.

'There's something we want to talk to you both about,' begins Mum, 'now that Amy is home. It's something that concerns us all and we want to know how you feel about it.'

Barker yawns, stretches and turns upside down in his bed, with his paws in the air, as if to make a point.

'Your mum and I think this would be a good time to move to a different area,' says Dad simply. 'Put the past behind us. Have a fresh start.'

I read between the lines. A move will spare me the pain of returning to senior school (eventually) without my best friend. And it will be a chance for us all to distance ourselves from the accident and isolate me from the attentions of the local press, who, says Mum, are keen to follow my story of 'courage'.

'Why do we have to move just because of her?' wails Caz. 'Before it happened, everything had to work round her and her training. She *always* comes first. You don't care about me and my happiness. I'm started my exam courses. And I've got Marcus...' She pushes back her chair and runs out of the kitchen, up the stairs and into her bedroom, slamming the door.

'That went well,' says Dad, putting his head in his hands.

'Where would we move to?' I ask gingerly, imagining the horror of being marooned on a remote Scottish island, with only seals and otters for company.

'Brighton,' replies Dad. 'I've got work contacts there. And there's a fantastic art college for Mum. Two universities. And great schools for you girls. It's very bohemian. Lots of cafés and theatres and designer shops. And best of all, there's the sea. You've always wanted to learn how to sail.'

That was before, Dad. The closest I'll get to the water now is the role of Long John Silver in the Christmas panto...

'What do you think?' asks Mum, her hand resting on my arm.

'Could I still see Harry?' I blurt out.

Mum and Dad look at each other. 'Of course,' says Dad. 'No problem. Maybe he can come and stay.' I feel a thud as Mum kicks Dad under the table and covers it up by moving her chair.

'Then it's fine.' I shrug.

It's not fine – it's sprocky and terrible and I want to lose it completely and sob like a four-year-old, but there's something telling me that change will be good. I'm going to be disabled wherever I go, so maybe the seaside isn't a bad option.

'I'll go and speak to your sister,' says Mum gently. 'See if some bribery about riding lessons doesn't do the trick.'

'It might take a while to sell this place,' says Dad, making conversation. He's not looking at me, but at the candles. 'But that will give you time to get well and strong again. If I could wave a magic wand and make it happen straight away, Amy, I would. Then you wouldn't have to see that wretched crossing, or the pool, ever again.'

I haven't even thought about what it would be like to drive past the monuments of my old life. I've been more interested in surviving, step by step, day by day.

Dad helps himself to a beer from the fridge. He throws a newspaper onto the kitchen table from beside the sink and says quietly, 'You may want to read this.'

There is a photo of Sophie on the front page under the headline: 'Suspended sentence for killer driver'. The short text informs me that 'Reginald Ambler (46) of Priory Avenue, Newcastle', has been given a 'six-month suspended prison sentence and a fine of £500 for failing to stop at a crossing in Nottingham city centre on 6 July, resulting in the accidental death of Sophie Haynes (13) and the maiming of her best friend and record-breaking swimmer Amy Curtis (13)'. The story continues inside, but I don't want to look at it.

'What does "suspended" mean, Dad?' I ask.

'It means he won't have to serve any of it, unless he ever does something like this again.'

'But he killed Sophie,' I whisper. 'He was on the phone…'

'The law calls that careless. He said he was very sorry in court.'

'You went to the trial?' So Dad has secrets too. I wish he'd stop treating me like a little kid. It's not as if I can forget all about it if I don't know what's going on. Every time I hear the scraping of metal I hold my breath…

'I wanted to look into the face of the man who hurt my girl and got away with it,' says Dad, simply. And I notice the hand that is holding the small bottle is shaking.

'Was Shirley there?' I ask.

Dad nods. 'And Gus.'

'How were they?' I persist.

'It was a terrible day for all of us,' is all Dad says, draining his beer. I feel like there is something he's not telling me.

I look at the paper again, at the picture of my friend in her school uniform, grinning from ear to ear. Her face is so familiar – I know every contour of it. And now, it will never change, never drink champagne, never be kissed, never be full of the joy of success or the sadness of disappointment, never see foreign lands or cry over stupid movies, never again make me laugh with its mad expressions.

Never is a long time, Soph…

While I am digesting this, my eyes are drawn back to the headline of a smaller article at the bottom of the page. It reads: 'Local swimmer sets new record', and it's accompanied by ! photo of Mel James at the Nationals. 'Watch your back,' she had said to me. 'Double whammy,' as Harry would say. I feel like someone has put a knife in my heart and twisted it. And in that moment, a question which has loomed heavily in my consciousness is answered.

'Dad,' I begin, but my voice is wavering. 'The team dinner – I can't…'

'You don't have to go. I can let Dan know. He'll understand…' says Dad, perplexed that my mind has made this random leap.

'It's because of this.' I point to the paper, trying to explain.

'Amy…' says Dad, moving quickly to the chair next to me, sitting and enveloping me with his arms, containing my sobs with his shoulder. 'It's unjust and terrible, I know. People should pay the price for what they do.'

I already have, Dad. The evidence is here, in black and white…

From: **amycurtis@ntlworld.com**

To: **rabidralph@hotmail.com**

Subject: **Home sweet home**

Dear Poppikins,

Well, I'm home, and in some ways it's great and in other ways it's awful and I wish I was back in the ward having a laugh with you. There's a lot of news — some kid broke my swimming record. I'm depressed! We're moving to Brighton on the south coast (Caz is suicidal because of Marcus). The lorry driver didn't have to go to prison. So he's still driving lorries and probably running kids over on crossings. Write to me soon, pleeeeez, and tell me all the news. Say hi to everyone for me. Hope you're OK.

Lamey

17

'Amy? Time to go,' calls Mum.

I'm lying on my bed, which is where I've spent most of the last two weeks, when I haven't been walking up and down the garden and terrorising the local cats with my crutches. Bed feels safe. It's the only place my body doesn't ache.

Today I get my new leg. And that means I can see Harry. I'm really annoyed that he hasn't replied to my emails. I've written to him every day. Maybe the computer in the Day Room has blown up? I won't let my brain think about the other reasons there could be for his silence.

Mum's waiting for me downstairs. She's got a sparkly clip in her hair and looks really pretty.

'Ready, then?' She smiles. She's being extra cheerful, which is always a worry. Her eyes miss nothing. They've spotted the raspberry stain on my trousers. Luckily, it's too late to go and change.

It's a beautiful September day. Bees and butterflies are moving lazily between flowers. Caz is at school. (She did try to skive off after an unfortunate accident with a wash-in hair dye, which has turned her blonde mane pale green, but Mum wasn't sympathetic.) Barker is sunbathing upside down on our front porch. And a blackbird is singing his end-of-summer song perched on the 'For Sale' sign in our flower border.

We've had quite a few people round. After the first lot, the estate agent – a man with oily skin and gelled hair – suggested to Mum that leaving my false leg in the middle of my bedroom was 'likely to put off prospective purchasers'.

There's been one firm offer – from the Suggs family. Mum and Dad are thinking about it because it's £5,000 under the asking price. They're borrowing quite a bit from the bank to move south. I've seen a picture of the new house. It's a Victorian semi opposite a small park. The walls are white and there's a purple creeping plant growing round the front door. There are four bedrooms. The smallest will be Dad's office – he's going to work from home as a freelance architect.

'Hop in,' says Mum, without thinking. 'Sorry, Amy…'

I put my crutches on the back seat and slide in after them. I feel nervous sitting in the front passenger seat after the accident. It feels safer in the back and further away from the approaching traffic…

It takes about half an hour to drive to the hospital. I notice how the leaves are turning red and gold and how the pavements are strewn with the first conkers. And I realise, as we approach the large car park, that my heart is beating faster than usual…

We're early for my appointment and I ask Mum if I can see Harry first. She agrees on condition she can go to the garden and have a cigarette. I make my way to Sunflower Ward, along the corridor where Harry took me for a ride on his wheelchair. There's a strong smell of disinfectant as I approach Sister Beresford's office.

I decide not to report in, but to arrive unannounced at Harry's bed. As I approach, I see that he is asleep, with the sheet over his head. I don't recognise the cards on his bedside table.

'Harry?' I say softly.

'He gone, that naughty Harry,' says a deep voice from behind me. Isabella crosses herself, clutches her mop handle and casts her eyes to the ground. Sister Beresford has seen me and is bustling over, concerned.

'Gone where?' I ask her, dreading the answer. My whole body is suddenly trembling.

'London, dear. Guy's Hospital. There's a new drug. Harry's been selected for treatment. The results could benefit thousands of children.' Sister Beresford takes my arm to steady me. I must be swaying.

I look into her kind eyes and imagine Harry strung up near the ceiling by his arms, being lowered into a vat of bubbling liquid that has 'Miracle Cure' on the side of it. He's screaming, 'Don't make me disappear!' Moments later, all that remains of him is Ralph, the racoon hat, floating on the surface.

'What a pity you missed him,' says Sister Beresford gently. 'You look so well, Amy. I know he would have loved to have seen you.'

'When will he be back?' I ask frantically.

'Not for a long, long time…' mutters Isabella, crossing herself again.

'We don't have a date, dear. I'm sure he'll be in touch very soon…' She puts her arm round me and guides me towards the double doors. 'It's so lovely to see you, Amy. Pop in anytime.'

And suddenly, I am walking with my crutches back up the corridor with angry strides. Mum is only halfway through her cigarette on the bench in the garden when I arrive. I feel I am going to explode with anger. Boris is smirking in his new position by the side of the gravel path. I take aim and smash him to pieces with my left crutch, hoping there are no frogs lurking near his rod.

'I've always hated that gnome,' I say. A small girl with her leg in plaster who is sitting on the next bench starts to cry. Mum quickly stubs out her cigarette and ushers me inside.

'God, Amy…' she keeps saying, lost for words.

I want to say, 'He had it coming,' but when Mum speaks in a quiet voice you know she is mean and dangerous. She tells me I must replace it out of my pocket money. I am already thinking I might treat the hospital garden to a Bambi instead.

'Time to meet your new leg,' says Ed triumphantly in the grotto. It's a strange way of putting it, but then this is someone who makes spare body parts for a living.

'Ta-daa,' he announces, unveiling my special limb on his workbench. It looks sleek and beautifully moulded. He demonstrates the ankle joint, which is smooth and silent. He shows me how the straps work.

I don't want it, I don't want any of this...

'It's made from Pelite – a foam plastic. Let's try it on.' Ed beams.

Mum helps me slip off my trousers, and I sit down to undo the buckles on Barbie for the last time. The new leg fits snugly onto my stump. It feels cool against my skin. Ed tightens the straps above my knee.

'The moment of truth,' he says quietly and motions for me to stand up. I take a deep breath and thrust my body forward, taking my weight on both my legs.

'How does it feel?' he asks.

I attempt a few paces, very slowly. The limb is light and responsive, but unreal. It's like walking when you've got cramp in your calf muscles and your leg feels like it belongs to someone else.

'Try without the crutches, if you like,' suggests Ed. I give them to Mum, who is biting her bottom lip so hard it's leaving a sort of rabbit-tooth imprint.

Here goes. First of all, balance, Amy. I have my arms out like a trapeze artist. Brain, are we going to do this or what? I know how Neil Armstrong must have been feeling when he was about to take the first walk on the moon, with the eyes of the world watching his every gesture. One giant leap for mankind. That's where the similarity ends, though...

I force myself to gulp a deep breath and as I exhale I move my right leg forward just a few inches, taking my weight on it, following through with my left leg. The action resembles an exaggerated limp. I manage two more shaky steps before wimping out and asking Mum for my crutches.

I won't be a clown for ever, Harry...

'It's great,' I say, truthfully, surprised by the comfort of the fit. My murderous instincts have calmed now. Maybe my new limb and I can learn to be friends. 'Thanks so much, Ed,' I say, giving him a big hug.

'You'll need others as you grow,' he explains, 'so by the time you're eighteen, we'll be old mates.'

I'm filled with a surging panic. 'But we're moving to Brighton and it'll be too far to come.' Hadn't Mum and Dad realised that I would need regular help from Ed and his team?

Ed looks disappointed. 'In that case, you'll have to send me a postcard and let me know how it's going,' he says brightly. 'There's an excellent rehab centre there. You'll be in good hands.'

Mum and I are silent on the journey home. She's still in shock that her daughter is a gnome-murderer. I'm sad

I can't show Harry my new leg, or hear him tell me that everything's going to be all right, the way he always does. Maybe I can take a digital picture with Dad's camera and load it onto my computer to send by email...

When we reach our road, there is an ambulance outside our house.

'What in heaven's name...?' shrieks Mum, jamming on the brakes in the drive and flying out of the driver's seat.

It takes me a little longer to reach the hallway, in time to see two hunky paramedics bending over Caz, who is sitting on a chair in the kitchen. She looks like Princess Leia from *Star Wars*, with two bulbous lumps on her ears. The lumps consist of bandages, not hair, though.

'I wanted my ears pierced for my birthday,' she is wailing to Mum. 'Marcus has bought me really expensive earrings...'

'We've told her it would have been safer to go to a salon,' says the taller paramedic, whose name, according to his badge, is Sam. 'At least she had the sense to call 999. It's made a bit of a mess of your sink though, Mrs Curtis.'

Mum is motioning for me to go upstairs. I'm happy to oblige. There's been enough blood spilled for one day. I decide I'll try and go up the normal way, using my feet and not my bum. I'm doing fine. I want to shout, 'Hey everyone, I'm doing it on my own,' but it's not the right time.

Downstairs, Princess Leia is getting what's coming to her from Darth Vader...

Sprockykins,

I think you are being held against your will in a London laboratory and used in sinister experiments to find a cure for baldness. Why haven't you replied to my emails? Did you get the picture of my new leg? Coolio, isn't it? Am worried you have now been abducted by aliens. Please write, or ring me, 'cos I could do with some jokes, even yours, which shows you how desperate I must be. Am sending this letter to your home in case your Hotmail has exploded. Hope you are OK.

Lamey

18

Mum's read a lot of books about 'confronting your demons' – the things in life which frighten you or make you unhappy, and today I've decided that the time has come for me to put their advice – that it's better to do something than nothing – to the test.

Every time I've raised the subject of Shirley and Gus at home, Mum and Dad have become vague and weird. They've more or less said that it's up to Shirley to make contact with us and if she hasn't, it means she needs her 'space', or more time to 'mend'.

Surely, if a friend is in pain, you go and see what you can do to help? Mum has always been fantastic at that sort of thing. We never seem to go anywhere without Mum having to drop off a bunch of flowers or some choccies with x, y or z who has been having a horrible day/week/life.

I'm beginning to think Shirley doesn't like me anymore and Mum and Dad are just protecting me from the truth…

But today is Shirley's birthday and normally we would take her a present. I don't want things to be more different than they are already, so I asked Mum if we could buy her some special biscuits. I've wrapped them up in red foil with a bow and made a card on the computer, which we've all signed.

Last year, Sophie and Gus made a cake with lots of cream in it and Shirley wore a flashing birthday badge to the picnic they had organised. I'm thinking there won't be much celebrating going on this time. The sky is like lead and stormy winds are blowing the car around. Dad's driving me over to the flat now. He and Mum argued about who should do it. Mum said he shouldn't 'dodge difficult emotional situations' all the time. I noticed he didn't say goodbye to her.

I haven't brought my crutches, so Dad's having to lend me his arm so that I don't fall on the drenched concrete path that leads to the block of flats. The wide entrance door is missing its glass today – the victim of vandalism. The hallway has been freshly painted, though – a nice cream colour. One of the ground-floor residents has put a vase with red plastic flowers on a small table outside their door. The flowers look a bit sad covered in raindrops that have blown in and soaked the floor.

We have to climb two flights of stairs. I take it slowly, holding on to the rail. Dad walks behind me, lost in thought. Perhaps he is remembering the last time he was here, just as summer was starting, when he tried to tap-dance down these steps like Gene Kelly.

We're not singing in the rain today.

We knock on the door of number twelve. After quite

a long time, Shirley answers. Her face is much thinner than I remember, with lots of lines, and her brown hair has two inches of grey at the roots. She's wearing a long, black cardigan over dark trousers – the sunny rainbow tie-dyes have gone. Worst of all, she doesn't ask us in, even though I phoned to ask if we could pop over. She just stands in the doorway, looking at us. The TV is on in the lounge. The white light from the screen creates shadows on the hall wall.

The first door on the right is firmly closed. The hand-drawn sign on it reads 'Sophie's room. Do not enter.' I long to turn the handle and smell Sophie's familiar smell.

'Hi, Shirley,' I say brightly. 'Happy birthday.'

'Hello, Amy, love,' she says, gently. She nods formally at my dad who nods back. What's with all this nodding? Dad's shuffling his feet and obviously wants to scarper. I wish Mum were here. She always knows what to do in these situations.

I give Shirley the special tin of biscuits and lean forward to give her a kiss.

'So you're going, then?' she says, stopping me.

'Once the sale goes through,' replies Dad, trying to sound cheerful. 'We'll keep in touch, though. Ellen thought you and Gus might like to come for a holiday in Brighton…'

'Thanks,' she answers, coolly. I want to shake the pair of them.

'Right then. We'll, um…' Dad is making our excuses. This will be the shortest visit in the history of time.

'I've got something for you, Amy,' Shirley says quietly and disappears behind her door. Dad and I exchange glances. When she returns, she's clutching a photo of Sophie and me dressed up for the Hallowe'en party at school last year. We're wearing pumpkin suits – orange sweatshirts discovered in charity shops, stuffed with pillows.

'Found it in her drawer. Thought you should have it,' says Shirley.

'Thank you,' I whisper, slightly choked. Dad puts his arm round me. I want to ask her why she didn't come to the hospital in all those weeks. And to tell her that I miss Sophie so much. And I'm so terribly sorry...

'Turn that ruddy telly down,' Shirley suddenly yells. The volume decreases instantly. The screen images still flicker in the darkness. 'Little git,' she mutters.

I'd almost forgotten about Gus. I wonder why he hasn't said hello. I'm not sure whether I should call out to him. From the look on Shirley's face, there seems to be nothing more to say.

'Bye then,' I murmur and just as we are moving off, she grabs me by the shoulders and gives me a big, warm hug. Her hair smells musty, like an old bird's nest.

'It's a crying shame,' is all she says, before retreating into her flat and closing the door.

Dad and I sit in silence in the car. Fat water droplets run in rivulets down the windscreen, distorting the outside world. Colours from the curtains in the flats mix with the street lights and make psychedelic patterns.

'Purple rain,' sighs Dad, lost in thought. Then he turns to me. 'I'm sorry for what went on in there, Amy. Shirley's upset with me because of what happened in court.'

'What do you mean?' I ask.

'She caused a bit of a scene when the sentence was passed on Reginald Ambler. I tried to calm her down, but she wouldn't stop shouting. I took her outside for some air. She was yelling at me as if I'd done it... Then he came out of court and walked past us without saying a word. Shirley tried to attack him. Anyway, the police sorted it out and got her a doctor. Gus was obviously in a bit of a state too. She wouldn't let me drive them home...'

Oh Soph, you won't believe the damage...

'It's like a Gehry landscape,' says Dad quietly, staring at the drenched urban street beyond the windscreen. 'The architect who designed the Guggenheim Museum in Bilbao. Strange shapes and jagged edges. No straight lines.'

He starts the engine and the wipers clear our vision. As we pull away, I look up at Sophie's flat and see that Gus is watching us out of the window, from behind the cream net curtain. I wave, but he doesn't wave back. Maybe he can't see through the rain...

~

Mum has steaming soup ready for us when we arrive home. I eat mine quietly at the kitchen table. Dad makes

Barker do tricks for some squirty cream, dangled tantalisingly above his gullible head.

'How's Shirley?' asks Mum, forcefully taking the can of cream out of Dad's hand and putting it back in the fridge with a warning stare. 'Dog diet, remember?' she mouths at him, pointedly. He sits down on his haunches next to Barker and pretends to sulk. Mum doesn't respond. She seems fed up with Dad's antics.

'Weird,' I answer, not looking up. I'd rather Dad tell her about it later.

'Goodbyes are always hard. And every time she sees you, she must think…' Mum's voice trails off.

'Think what?' I press her.

'That we are the lucky ones. That life is so unfair.'

I remember Shirley's hug. There was genuine love in it, not anger. Mum's got her wrong. Shirley may not live in a tree-lined road or be lucky enough to have a new car and holidays in France. But she is warm and kind, and hurting.

The phone is ringing. Caz answers and hands it to me, shrugging. My eyes widen. Harry?

'Hi?' I say. There is the sound of heavy breathing.

'Is that Amy?' asks a young, confident female voice.

'Yeah,' I say, puzzled.

'It's Sorcha. Harry's sister.'

I can hear other young voices in the background and the intermittent sound of canned laughter from a television.

'Harry wrote you a message and I put it inside my crisp

packet so I wouldn't lose it and Mum threw it away, but I found it again and it's all yucky with tomato soup and cat food and stuff but I'm going to read it to you, OK?'

'Yes,' I reply, reduced to monosyllables, suddenly paranoid that Harry is too ill to speak to me himself.

'"*Lam*eee,"' begins Sorcha, stressing the wrong syllable.

'Lamey,' I correct her.

She sighs and tuts. '"Lamey, they are torturing me here in London. Alert Amnesty International and the Home Secretary to secure my immediate release. Actually, don't. There's a mega-spangly nurse here called Flavia who has really fit legs and she does the can-can just for me. OK, that's just in my dream. I'm on very strong drugs which make me hallucinate all the time. Saw that photo of you and your new Barbie and thought you were quite good-looking, so that proves my point. Howzit going in the real world, then? I'm confined to bed for bad behaviour indefinitely, so don't email. Write to me soon, you limbless lump. Ward Eight. Oncology. Guy's Hospital. London. Harry."' Sorcha, who has delivered this in a monotone, clears her throat.

'Is Harry very ill?' I ask the reluctant news-bearer.

'He died last week. Sort of. Then he got better,' she replies, matter-of-factly.

My heart is suddenly in my mouth. 'Sorcha, can I please speak to your mum?'

'In the bath. Got to go now. Bye.' And she's gone.

Mum takes one look at my shocked white face and immediately goes into action. We find the number for Guy's Hospital from directory enquiries and Mum gets through to the Oncology reception.

'Yes, hello,' says Mum. 'I'm wondering if you could put me through to one of your patients please – Harry Higgins, Ward Eight. Thank you.' She crosses her fingers. A minute passes. I hear the same voice again. Mum is nodding. 'He's sleeping,' she says to me in a whisper. 'I see. Thank you. Um, is it possible to leave a message for him? From my daughter Amy.'

God, what can I say that won't sound naff and pathetic?

'Stop being a drama queen and get out of there,' I say.

Mum looks a bit taken aback, and raises her eyebrows as if to say, 'Are you sure?' I nod my confirmation and so she repeats these words into the receiver, adding, 'They're great friends. Always teasing each other.'

'He's going to be fine,' I say, as Mum puts the receiver on the table gently and holds my hands. 'He's got to be.'

19

I'm waiting for the postman, like I do every day (I have to time him walking up and down the path – it's an Amy thing), because I know that by now Harry will have got my letter and had time to reply. When postman Quiche (whose real name is Keith, but Caz and I couldn't say that when we were little) strides up to our door and puts the letters through the letter box, I notice something bright and colourful amongst the usual bills and brown envelopes.

A postcard with a picture of the London Eye on it, addressed to me. An arrow is pointing to one of the pods high in the air and some scrawly writing says, 'Human guinea pig tests new vertigo-aversion therapy.'

Harry.

On the back, there are just three lines and my address: 'Dear Lamey, Can confirm, not dead – thanks for message. H.'

The day suddenly seems a lot brighter.

We're going to see Sophie today – or at least, where she is buried. Mum thinks it's a good idea for me to have a chance to see where she is lying. It will be my last goodbye. I've already given final hugs to Dan and the team, my teacher Miss Gates (who has been bombarding me with coursework notes and homework in all my subjects) and my mates from school. I'm all hugged out.

We've brought some pink cyclamens in pots to put on her grave. Hopefully, they'll flower until the spring. They were flowers which always made Sophie laugh. She called them 'sick lemons'.

I'm glad it's so bright and sunny. Mum and I are both wearing sunglasses, which is weird for October. The cemetery is in the grounds of St. Christopher's Catholic Church on the outskirts of town. Mum says she didn't know the Haynes family were religious until the funeral. I remember Shirley has a cross on the wall above the gas fire in the lounge, and that Sophie said her parents weren't divorced: a) because they weren't allowed to and b) because Shirley couldn't find Sophie's dad to divorce him.

I thought we told each other everything.

I didn't know she was a Catholic and believed in the Bible and stuff. She was always saying, 'Oh God, Amy!' and never prayed with her eyes shut in assembly at school. In fact she was the one who changed the words to 'Morning Has Broken' to 'Yawning and Choking' and 'Glad that I live am I, that the sky is blue' to 'Glad that I have one eye, so I can't see you'.

I miss her making me laugh.

Mum and I walk with linked arms along the gravel paths that criss-cross the cemetery. The cyclamens dangle in a carrier bag from Mum's right arm. Some of the gravestones are so old you can't read the words on them any more. There are quite a few huge stone tombs with whole families inside, which is spooky. Some have stone eagles with outstretched wings on top. They look like they will peck out your eyes.

Many of the graves are overgrown, like that of 'Billy Tyler, Aged 19, Beloved Son of Ena and Edward, Died on the Battlefield of the Somme in 1916. Marbles Champion of Warsop 1912–13.'

'His relatives have probably died or moved away by now,' says Mum, 'so there's no one to tend the grave.'

Poor Billy. I wonder what happened to his marbles?

Sophie is in the far right corner next to an evergreen hedge. Two sparrows are hopping about near the headstone. They fly off as we approach, alerted by the sound of my crutches scraping on the gravel.

Mum says she'll just go and look at the paintings in the church, which is great, as I want to be alone with Sophie for a little while. Mum walks away quietly. My stump is twingeing and I transfer my weight onto my left leg. I feel strangely embarrassed, standing here. Embarrassed that I haven't had the courage to come before. Embarrassed that I'm disabled. That I'm the one who survived.

I'm not sure what I expected, but nothing is happening. Sophie's not chirping, 'What took you so long?' or, 'Oh God, what happened to your leg?' She's not grabbing my crutches and saying 'They're really cool, can I have a go?' or even, 'Let's get out of here.'

Silence, apart from sweet birdsong. Did you want a fanfare of trumpets, Amy? What kind of an idiot talks to a grave?

It's weird, but something strange happens to you when you're in the presence of the dead. You do things very quietly, as if any sudden noise or movement will disturb their peace. I bend down to arrange the four pots of cyclamens next to her headstone. There are some yellow flowers here already, which have wilted, pecked about by tiny beaks looking for grubs. Next to them is a small brown teddy, his hair matted and tatty after four months in the elements. I recognise him as Treacle, whom Sophie took to bed each night. I try to smooth his hairy face, give him a kiss and replace him gently.

After a time, I force myself to look up at the words under the dates on Sophie's headstone. They read:

IN LOVING MEMORY OF
SOPHIE HAYNES, AGED 13,
A DAUGHTER TO SHIRLEY AND SISTER TO GUS
KEEP ON RUNNING AND BE FREE
OUR GIRL

It's true then. She really is here, under the ground.

I wish they had said something about Sophie winning the 1,500-metres at our last sports day, because in time to come, there will be no relatives to remember her achievements and strangers will pass by, unaware that she had been a champion.

I wonder what mine will say one day?

I think everyone should have a stone that lists the highlights of their lives. Even animals. 'Here Lies Barker, Much Loved Pet of the Curtis Family. In his lifetime, he ate 2,000 lipsticks and 450 envelopes…'

The sun is warm on my face. I lean against the headstone and close my eyes, feeling much less scared now. This isn't such a frightening place to come. I was going to say something to Soph about never forgetting her, but in the peaceful stillness, it doesn't seem to matter. It sounds corny, but I feel her everywhere. She isn't just in the earth. My thoughts are mingling with her just as my memories of her are alive and jigging about in my mind.

I'm not leaving you, Soph. You'll always be with me.

When I open my eyes, Mum's standing there, smiling at me. Shafts of sunlight surround her and make her glow. She looks like an angel. She offers me her hand to help me up.

'Did you like the paintings?' I ask.

'Too many Madonnas,' she says, turning up her nose. 'I lit a candle for Sophie and asked them all to keep an eye on her.' Mum winks at me. I love it that she can be funny about serious things. We walk along the gravel paths towards the car and a blackbird hops along beside us, occasionally stopping to pluck a worm from the ground. It flies up onto the arched gate by the road and chirps a fantastic song.

And suddenly I hear, carried on the breeze, swirling across the trees and fields, tumbling over the gates and hedgerows…Sophie's laugh, loud and unmistakable. I think Mum hears it too. We exchange glances.

'See you later, alligator,' I shout, at the top of my voice.

The peaks and moors and white waterfalls, the grey stones of the villages, the winter fields lying stony and bare, the smoke from a hundred chimney pots and the steam from the cattle eating hay in the barns all answer together: 'In a while, crocodile …'

~

From: amycurtis@ntlworld.com
To: rabidralph@hotmail.com
Subject: Boxes

Hi Poppikins,

Thanks for your card. You had me worried for a while… What are they doing to you in London? I want ALL the details. The Eye looks great. When we live in Brighton, Dad says it's only forty-seven minutes by train to London, so we can come and do the sights. I'll come and see you if you want, although I'd have to fit you in after the Natural

History Museum and the Hard Rock Café.

There are boxes everywhere and Barker is shredding the newspaper we're using to wrap things in. My life has fitted into four crates. Caz has seven. (One of these is just for love letters from Marcus — ugh!) I can't believe we're leaving here tomorrow. Hope you are getting better. Don't worry about replying because Dad is going to pack up the computer tonight so the next time I email will be from Brighton!

BFN

Lamey

From: **rabidralph@hotmail.com**

To: **amycurtis@ntlworld.com**

Subject: **Re: Boxes**

Lamey,

Thanks for message. I just came to check my Hotmail — spooky! Am very bored — currently in a room on my own due to:

a) the offensive colour of my new pyjamas (lime-green parrots). Blame Mum.

b) my 'moral depravity' (won £20 off the nurses playing cheat).

c) Ralph (tried to bite the oncologist and is now quarantined, although the RSPCA is fighting his case).

So visiting just now might be tricky. You'd probably have more fun at Madame Tussauds — the waxworks look more alive than this lot here. The end of the month might be better, as by then, Ralph and I should be back in circulation.

Good luck with the move. Send me pics of the new pad.

Harry

20

'Those are the South Downs,' says Mum, as we approach a line of hills stretching across the horizon.

I blink my eyes open. I've been asleep since we left Nottingham. Now the landscape is completely different.

'They run from Winchester to Eastbourne – about eighty miles,' she adds. ' I walked the whole thing once, with a boyfriend from art college. We lived on baked bean sandwiches.'

Caz and I exchange glances. It's hard to think of Mum living rough. It does explain her violent dislike of baked beans, though.

Caz still has red-rimmed eyes. Her parting with Marcus by our gatepost, involving lots of snogging and nose-blowing was, in her words, 'very traumatic'.

There are rabbits hopping about on the roundabout at the entrance to the city of Brighton and Hove and loads of parks everywhere, with big houses overlooking them. Dad opens his window and we smell the sea. Gulls peck at the rubbish bins outside cafés. A limousine car with tinted windows (the sort film stars travel in) purrs past us in the opposite direction. A young man with dirty hair is sitting in a sleeping bag in a shop doorway, begging for money.

'I think that's terrible,' says Caz. 'The police should take him away.'

Five minutes later, we're parking in our new driveway, outside the house whose picture we've studied for the last two months. It looks tattier than in the photo, which was taken in the summer, when all the flowers were vibrant with colour. Dead things hang over the edge of terracotta pots and the border by the front path is full of brown weeds.

Caz has already bagged the bedroom overlooking the park and is sitting defiantly on her bed, determined not to move.

I'm really happy to have the smaller room at the back – you can see the pond in the walled garden from the window, and it's east-facing, which means I can watch the sun rise, an old habit from my past life. There are blue curtains with dogs on, left behind by the previous owners and a poster of a Golden Retriever still inside the door of the built-in wardrobe. They must have been nice people.

I take some pictures with Dad's digital camera so that I can scan them later and send them to Harry, in the hope he'll access his Hotmail again. While the removal men unload our furniture, I sit on the low wall in the front garden and take lots of angles of the front of the building, with its tall sash windows and white walls covered in that climbing plant. Mum says it's wisteria. Dad said that's what Caz is suffering from. Ha, ha. Not.

I can hear Barker clattering about on the polished wooden floors, his feet slipping from under him each time he goes round a corner. When he barks, it echoes round the house.

Caz is not so easily impressed. 'I hate it,' she says simply, flouncing past me and getting back into the car, where she promptly bursts into tears.

It's late now – a starry, starry night (Mum's favourite song). I'm eating chips in the back garden, watching Barker watching the fish in the pond. The air is full of incense, which is wafting over from next door's meditation session. Faint strains of a saxophone drift across the dark park. The new moon smiles at me, like a shining toenail. A bat dances round my head and swoops off into a tall tree. It's cool here, I think as I go inside.

Mum has made up my bed and put my toothbrush and toothpaste on the blue basin in the corner. We all have our own basins now – Dad says this is an advantage of a Victorian house. I take a last look out of the window. Barker is still staring at the fish. His head is moving in slow motion, following their progress round the pond. His ears are bent forward, and the tip of his big, hairy tail is wagging, like it always does when he thinks he knows something and you don't. He has obviously appointed himself Chief Guardian of the Fish, which is a promotion from Chief Lipstick Chomper.

I close my unfamiliar dog curtains, sit down on the side of my bed, wriggle out of my jeans and unstrap my leg, putting it tidily next to my bedside table. It still has its sock on and looks a bit weird. Mum has complained recently that I leave it lying around on the floor and 'one of these days, someone will fall over it and hurt themselves'. She looks immediately guilty when she says this, aware that she is using the same tone that she employs when telling Barker off for leaving his squeaky bones about.

'I would rather not have to take it off, Mum,' I say, hurt.

'I'm so… Oh Amy,' she whispers, enveloping me in her arms. I realise that maybe Mum is coping less well with the concept of my real leg being absent than I am.

You never expect to have to tidy your own legs up when you are thirteen…

21

From: rabidralph@hotmail.com

To: amycurtis@ntlworld.com

Subject: Curtis Towers

Dear Lamey,

New house looks coolio. Maybe I'll visit — when
your sprocky sister's out! I'll get my mum to post
me, as I am now only 0.5 centimetres tall — the
machine they're using to zap Trevor has unfortunate
side effects. Will save a fortune on rail fares.
Mind the seagulls don't peck out your eyes. Am
attaching Christmas list so that you have plenty of
time to get my presents!

Harry

From: amycurtis@ntlworld.com

To: rabidralph@hotmail.com

Subject: Re: Curtis Towers

Dear Poppikins,

Have looked at your list, but feel that opportunities
for using a snowboard in Nottingham are limited. And
tropical fish would be difficult to send. But there

```
is a great Sea Life Centre here, so you might like
to come and do the 'Walking With Sharks' tour with me?
Lamey
```

```
From:       rabidralph@hotmail.com
To:         amycurtis@ntlworld.com
Subject:    Curious
```

```
Since when did sharks have legs? Brighton sounds
a strange place.
H
```

~

It had to happen. I just wish it wasn't happening today.

Mum is insisting on taking me Christmas shopping. She says she's tired of seeing me in these old stretchy trousers and trainers. She has plans to revamp my wardrobe.

'But the shops will be really crowded, and there'll be that yucky music playing and all the shop assistants will be wearing stupid Santa hats…'

I've tried really hard to dampen her enthusiasm. But when Mum gets the bug to hit the High Street, there is no stopping her.

I haven't shown the world my new leg yet. I'm not ready to stand in a queue of other girls who are waiting to try on five sparkly Christmas dresses each. If they catch a glimpse of my straps in the mirror of my changing cubicle as they pass, they'll probably scream.

I try to explain this to Mum as we prepare to leave.

'If you're not self-conscious, no one will stare,' she suggests.

Yeah, right. As if the 2,000 people in the covered mall aren't going to notice my clown walk or look at my crutches.

The only good thing about this expedition is that, to get to the multi-storey car park, you have to drive along the seafront. There's a massive Christmas tree just in front of the entrance to the Brighton Pier, and kids skating on the temporary rink just in front of it. The winter tide is grey and heavy, with white horses leaping across it. Loads of joggers are running along the prom. Someone's flying a kite on the beach. A big, grey mongrel dog is galloping next to a man on a bike, keeping pace with him.

There are all kinds of people here. Most of them have two legs, though.

It takes ages to get a parking space because of the Christmas crowds. Mum is undeterred. She wants us to root round a big department store first. We arrive in a wide lift and emerge into a frenzy of shoppers. It's a special promotion day, and everything is reduced by twenty per cent.

All the kids in the 'Teen Wear' section are staring at me. It's difficult looking at the racks of clothes and holding my crutches. I pick out some stretchy blue trousers with a white stripe down the side and hope Mum will be pleased.

'They're not really smart, though, are they?' she says. 'You need some for going out.'

'Going out where?' I say, suspiciously.

'Parties and other people's houses,' she continues, vaguely.

Um. Hello? I don't have any friends here…

'I really, really like these trousers,' I state, emphatically.

'That's fine. But we didn't come all this way just for one pair,' says Mum, rifling through racks of narrow-legged jeans.

Before I know it, I am taking four pairs of trousers and three jumpers into the changing room. Mum is outside, waiting for me to come out and model them. I rest my crutches on the partition wall and take off my fleecy jacket. I have to sit down on the chair to undo my trainers. It's so clever how Ed has matched my false foot to my real one. Under my socks, they look just the same. I wiggle out of my jogging bottoms, stand up and take the first pair of trousers from the hook.

But then I see something quite shocking in the three mirrors in the cubicle, which give you a complete view of your body.

There is a girl with a scary stump strapped to a prosthetic limb. A girl who has lost her athletic shape and strong shoulders, who is a little overweight round her stomach and untidy in the hair department. A girl who has small breasts that look like they belong to someone else, growing under her ribbed sweater. And a bum that is spreading like a ripe peach...

The girl is me. I hardly recognise myself.

I sit down again, crushed by the terrible truth of my reflection. I am ugly, ugly, ugly.

The tears begin slowly at first, drizzling out of the corner of my eyes. But this isn't just a job for my tear ducts. My whole body is in mourning for itself, and soon joins in with heaving sobs.

A shop assistant who is doling out the plastic cards telling you how many garments you have loiters outside my curtain.

'Is everything all right in there?' she asks tentatively, before pushing back the blue material. She gasps at the sight of not just one false leg, but false legs stretching to infinity in the prism mirror helpfully designed to allow you to see multiple versions of yourself. 'I'm so sorry,' she whispers.

'So am I,' I wail. And then Mum comes to my rescue and gathers me up in her arms, closes the curtain and wipes my tears, all in one movement.

'I'm so hideous,' I gulp. 'I'm never going to like my body again. Never...'

Mum holds me tight until my chest stops convulsing. Then she takes my face in her hands and stares at me, very hard. 'Listen to me, Amy. At the moment, all you can see when you look in the mirror is what is missing. When I look at you, I see a beautiful young woman, with so much promise, and her whole wonderful life ahead of her...'

I nod. But deep down, I know mothers have to say those things. It's part of their job.

22

Dad is outside the front door when we reach home, looking excited. Before Mum can say anything about my traumatic incident, he asks me to close my eyes and he leads me indoors. There's a strong smell of pine forests.

'Open!' he says.

It's a huge Christmas tree, covered in white fairy lights. It must be over two metres tall. It reaches right up to the high ceiling in our hall. I hug Dad hard. It's better than ten pairs of stupid trousers.

'Put on a decoration and make a wish,' says Mum, offering me the box of lurid baubles, homemade stars and multi-coloured tinsel.

Caz appears from the kitchen and picks out a silver choirboy with a carol sheet. She clips him onto a branch. He immediately turns upside down, falls off and smashes on the floor.

'It's gravity,' says Dad, trying to console her. Actually, I think it has more to do with the wish I bet she was making – to see Marcus again and have him sing to her under the mistletoe. Fate is trying to tell her something.

'Decorating the tree's for babies, anyway,' she proclaims huffily.

Dad is staring at me. He has that look that says he is

going to prevent my decoration falling to the ground as enough of my life has already been broken into a thousand pieces.

I rummage round until I find the silver-and-blue bird with a soft white tail – my favourite piece in our whole wacky collection. Since I was three I've always been attracted to its pretty face and the feel of its fairy-soft plumage. Mum says it performs a magical song which none of us can hear. It only sings at Christmas, when it is set free to chirp in the celebrations.

Carefully, I clip it onto a branch midway up the tree. The fairy lights reflect off its scratched metal body. It seems to sway up and down with the motion of the disturbed pine needles.

'Make a wish,' whispers Dad, who has his eyes closed already.

It's always so hard, knowing what to wish for. World peace, an end to famine in Africa, the banning of all kinds of terrorism, mobile phones that play Mozart and those yucky smoky bacon crisps… And most of all, a message from Harry to say Trevor's gone for good.

And what about turning back time? Now that's a thought. Could a wish do that? Would that be a really selfish thing to ask for? And is being selfish always wrong? (When it is yourself you need to mend?)

'I'm going to save my wish,' I tell Dad, feeling defeated.

He nods and puts his hands on my shoulders.

'It's always good to have one up your sleeve,' he says, to make me feel better.

He bends down and motions for me to jump on his back, the way I used to when I was small. It isn't as hard as I think. My left leg is quite strong now and gives me a good upward spring. I hang on round his neck, screaming. He starts to gallop about, in and out of the lounge, the dining room, the kitchen, up and down the hallway... Barker joins in and woofs manically at us, skidding round corners in an effort to catch up.

Finally, Dad lowers me gently onto the stairs and lies there, puffing and laughing and groaning at the same time, between my feet. I notice how bald he's getting on the top of his head.

I wonder what Dad wished for. More hair, probably...

23

From: **amycurtis@ntlworld.com**

To: **rabidralph@hotmail.com**

Subject: **Parcel**

Hi Poppikins,

How r u? Haven't heard from you for a while, so
wonder if you and Ralph have escaped and are on
the run, which would be a shame, 'cos I've sent you
a parcel to help prevent you from becoming a boring
vegetable. I made the card with Dad's new PhotoShop
program. It took an hour to get Barker to sit still
with the hat on and then he yawned at the wrong
time, but Caz says it looks like he's singing
'Noël, Noël'. Anyway, happy Christmas.

Love,

Amy

From: **rabidralph@hotmail.com**

To: **amycurtis@ntlworld.com**

Subject: **Re: Parcel**

Hi Lamey,

Thanks for the spangly Sudoku book and card. Hope

you're having a Cool Yule. What's your best present?
Mine is — I'm home (surprise!). Had my first Coke
in a while today (threw up). The nurse I fancy gave
me a T-shirt with her picture on it. (It was top of
my Santa list, which I hung on the end of my bed!)
We can have a Sudoku match next time I see you.
You'll be rubbish, I expect. Happy New Year and
stuff, (We made it!).

Harry x

Christmas morning. There's frost on the grass in the park
and a clear, sharp, blue sky. But there's no phone call from
Sophie, who always used to ring pretending to be Santa.
She'd say, 'Ho, ho, ho,' through the cardboard centre of
a toilet roll, which made her voice sound deep and
masculine. We would open our stockings on our beds at
the same time, telling each other what presents we'd got.
Gus would bounce on her bed and beg to say ''lo, Ame,'
before being banished from her bedroom.

Do you celebrate Christmas in the other place, Soph?

I wonder what Shirley and Gus are doing this year.
They didn't send us a card, although I made one for them.
Maybe they just forgot to post ours in time.

We're all in the lounge — Mum, Dad, Caz, Barker and
I. There's a lovely fire in the grate and Mum has lit candles
that smell of cinnamon. I'm unwrapping my present from

Granny May in Ireland. Mum looks a bit tense and with good reason. It's a pair of toe socks. Mum goes pale. Caz has got the giggles. Dad's jaw drops in disbelief.

'You know she lives in a home and she's lost her marbles,' Mum explains, prising them from me, screwing them into a ball and putting them back into their paper.

My favourite family present is from Barker, who has given me a guitar (very generous) and a voucher for ten lessons.

Usually, he gives me a new swimming towel with a dog on it. This year, he decided a musical instrument that could be played while sitting down would be more appropriate. I hug him and say thank you.

'That's not fair,' Caz whines. 'He only gave me roller blades…' Mum shoots her a look which says, 'Zip your mouth,' which I'm not supposed to see.

Barker doesn't notice any of this, as he's chewing a new squeaky cat, which he has unwrapped with his teeth. He has already bitten its ear off.

My best present of all is from Harry, who has sent some special chocolates. 'Oooooh,' Mum and Caz say, exchanging glances as I unwrap them. My ears are flushing hot with embarrassment.

'How many kisses has he put in the card?' asks Caz, nosily.

'Three,' I answer, coolly.

'Three?' repeats Dad, surprised.

'Hooked up,' states Caz, triumphantly.

'No we're not. Shut up,' I say, sounding like a real brat. Mum's eyes are cautioning the others to leave it. Caz is smirking now. Even Mum has a grin playing round her lips.

Luckily for me, there's a distraction, in the form of mystery presents wrapped in blue, shimmery paper. It doesn't take us long to guess they have come from the fish in the pond, who, very generously, have given us tropical-blue dolphin T-shirts with plastic eyes that move (Dad says you can't expect fish to have good taste.)

Joan, our former neighbour, has sent us an embroidered hanky each with our initials in the corner. Unfortunately, she has muddled these up, so I've become 'A.G.' instead of 'A.E.' (Amy Ellen, after my mum). Cassandra Georgina is less than impressed and announces Joan has probably made them out of some old knickers. She has thrown hers in the bin. I keep mine, though, and tuck it under my pillow.

Caz is staring lovingly at the framed photo that Marcus has sent her. It shows him in full leathers, sitting astride a big motorbike (his brother's Harley), a cigarette drooping from his lips.

'I didn't know he smokes,' Mum says, disapprovingly.

'He doesn't,' Caz replies, defensively. 'He gave up when he met me.'

'Hmm,' says Mum, her lips pursed.

'It's not fair, you always criticise my friends. I'm not

doing DRUGS or SEX, so you should be happy,' she snaps, flouncing out of the room. Mum and Dad stare after her, mouths open. Then Dad pours himself a big brandy.

~

To cheer ourselves up, and help digest our veggie lunch, Dad has suggested a walk by the sea. We never normally go out on Christmas Day. It's a great idea. As always, there are loads of people everywhere. Mum sits with me on a bench on the promenade while Caz and Dad throw stones in the sea. Barker lies on the shingle, chewing dried cuttlefish.

Caz tries out her new roller blades and after a wobbly start hanging on to Dad's arm, seems to find some natural balance. She has stapled my toe socks together and is wearing them as a scarf to make me laugh. She can be OK, my sister. Most of the time, though, she is totally annoying. Mum says we're very different and will probably get on better when we're older.

The sun's beginning to set behind the pier, and a whole colony of starlings is swooping and diving around it, in perfect formation. The beaches are crowded with locals and visitors watching this beautiful dance. There are families, couples and loners – all of them out to take in the fresh sea air on this special day, all united in this moment in the airborne spectacle.

Close to shore, there's a crazy canoe club practising manoeuvres. The men wear tinsel on their helmets – one has a full Santa suit on. There are yachts on the horizon, almost looking like they aren't moving in the stillness of the afternoon.

Several photographers with massive zoom lenses are positioned near the old pier, trying to capture the last rays of light filtering through the iron structure. On the wide promenade, a unicyclist in a red jumper and French beret entertains children who are clutching balloons from McDonald's. Music from the carousel combines with electronic beeps and bells from the amusement arcades and drifts across the shingle and out to sea.

Two hours across the water, due south, French children are discussing their visit from Père Noël and playing with their new toys. Only two hours. Six months ago, I would have been able to swim that distance.

'I'm cold, Mum,' I say, as a shiver runs down my spine. It's nothing to do with the temperature, which feels much higher than in Nottingham. It's the realisation that I'll never feel the rush of the ocean against my skin again when I'm racing through the waves...

Mum insists on sticking the thermometer in my mouth when we get home. It reads 102 degrees. 'Straight to bed,' she orders.

And that's the end of Christmas. Except for one very unexpected event.

Mum and Dad are watching carols on the TV. They seem to be getting on better at the moment. Dad is singing along in his falsetto voice. Caz is telling him to shut up because she can't hear her new CD over 'Once in Royal David's City'. Now Mum is singing too – the descant bit about the angels – and the phone is ringing.

'Do I have to do everything?' I hear Caz grump, as she answers it in the hall. Next thing, she is standing in my bedroom doorway, holding the receiver in one hand and pointing at me.

'Who is it?' I whisper. My head is throbbing. I'm not capable of saying anything coherent.

'Won't say. Might be a heavy breather,' she says, throwing the receiver onto my bed and pulling a face.

I pick it up gingerly and hold it to my very hot ear. I suddenly realise, more than anything in the world, I want it to be Harry...

'Hello?' I hiccup, by mistake.

There's a sort of snuffling from the other end, like a nose being wiped on a sleeve, followed by a loud squeaking. Then silence.

'Hello?' I say again.

''lo, Ame.'

'Dollop? Hey, happy Christmas.'

More snuffling and squeaking.

'Got a guinea piggle from Santa,' says Gus softly.

'Have you? That's cool,' I reply. 'What's its name?'

'Colin,' he whispers.

'Why are you whispering, Dollop?' I ask. This all seems

so surreal, I wonder if I am actually delirious and imagining it.

''Cos he's asleep in my jim jams.'

'Don't move too quickly, then,' I advise.

'Not *wearing* them. Duh.' Gus is tutting to himself at my stupidity.

'Did you get lots of other pressies too?' I say, to fill the lengthening gap in the conversation.

'A cage and hay for Colin. Choccies – mmmmm. And some gel pens,' he wheezes. 'What did you get, Ame?'

'I got a guitar and some clothes and stuff,' I answer, not wanting to list the dozens of gifts stacked under the tree.

'Mega.'

That was one of Sophie's words. I can feel my throat tighten. 'Did you have turkey for lunch?' I manage to say.

'Nope. Burgers and chips.' He's giggling now.

'Are you teasing me, Dollop?'

'No, Ame. Mum said I could choose.'

'We had a nut roast,' I tell him.

'Yeuch,' splutters Gus.

'Are you watching telly, then?' I can hear canned laughter in the background.

'Nope. Watching Colin.' More giggles. 'Mum's having forty winks. Think she's had thirty-five so far. And guess what?'

'What?'

He forgets to whisper this time. 'She's still got her

paper hat on from that stupid cracker that didn't go BANG!'

Ouch, Gus, my head is already banging like a drum, thanks.

'Ame? Mum said I've got to make a Christmas wish.' He sighs.

'Right. Go on, then,' I encourage, rubbing my temples.

'Need a new sister. Miss Soph.' His voice is trembling.

'I can be your pretend sister if you like,' I offer. My eyes are stinging.

See what an empty space you have left in all our hearts, Soph?

There is a big sniff and a few moments' silence.

'Colin's waking up now,' whispers Gus. 'Got to make his dinner.'

'OK, Dollop. It was nice to talk to you.'

'Ame?'

'Yes?'

'Happy Christmas.'

24

It's January the sixth today. No emails from Harry. It's cold and windy. Mum's driving Caz to school. I'm in the back, on my way to my first appointment at the new rehab centre.

We've said goodbye to the old year with its traumas and sadness. Now it's 'last year' that I lost my best friend – and one of my essential body parts. It feels like yesterday. 'Time heals,' that's what everyone says. I think it just plays tricks on you, creating a false distance between you and the painful events of your life. The memories are imprinted on our cells for ever. I think I've got the January blues...

I have made two more resolutions – to be more tolerant of my big sister and make allowances for her shortcomings. And to be a feisty, don't-mess-with-me sort of babe. Mum is blaming my hormones for the latter. Personally, I can't see the link between my growing boobs and my new bolshiness, but Mum assures me it is quite normal, having consulted several gurus about puberty in the past. I've already worked out that the amount of bolshieness is not relative to size, as Caz is mega-bolshie and hers are like gnat bites.

We're pulling up outside an old red-brick hospital at the top of a very steep hill. Mum's staring at the large information board myopically. Arrows point left and right, according to the department you are destined for.

'Crocuses – spring's in a hurry,' she exclaims as we drive at twenty miles per hour along a narrow road which curves past the main building and rises steeply. The bright-yellow flower heads are uplifted towards the sun, triumphantly.

Outside the rehabilitation unit, a single-storey modern building, wooden troughs are full of pansies with pink and purple petals.

'Everything blooms so early here,' says Mum, almost to herself, as she pulls into an empty parking space opposite the entrance.

Inside, there's a wide reception area with a café. It's lovely and warm. Mum treats us both to a hot chocolate from a woman with blue hair and nose rings, whose name is Sammy.

Needless to say, there are a lot of the 'wide eyed and legless' club about. Not many kids – apart from an older girl who has lost her legs through meningitis, just like Harry, and is still in a wheelchair. My mum and her mum have struck up a conversation and talk about us both as if we're not here.

'I hate it when they do that,' says the girl, whose name is Beth. She can flip her chair round with one hand. Respect. She's chewing gum and wearing loads of eye make-up.

'Who're you seeing?' she asks, directly.

'Everyone. Physio, prosthetist…'

Beth is holding a Crunchie bar towards me.

'For courage,' she says.

I take it gratefully and am just about to unwrap it when a very tall, dark, athletic figure in jeans and a T-shirt moon-walks up to our table, giving me a big, stern stare, framed by masses of dreadlocks. He puffs his cheeks in and out and makes drumbeat sounds and then holds out his strong black hand. I give him mine. He grips it hard.

'Ramoul,' he says, beaming.

'Amy Curtis,' I reply, embarrassed that everyone in the room is looking at me, including Sammy, the girl with blue hair. I want the floor to swallow me up.

'Are you ready to enter my kingdom, Amy Curtis, and let me make your dreams come true?' he asks, glancing sideways at my mum, who is smiling at him, girlishly.

'OK.' I shrug. Why couldn't I have had a normal physio? Why does mine have to be a cross between Eddie Murphy and Scooby Doo?

'Then follow me to a brave new world,' he motions, his six-foot frame loping towards a pair of double doors.

As Mum and I get near his office, the sound of drums vibrates in the corridor. Ramoul is already sitting down in the Caribbean-blue-painted room, beckoning me in, making his own percussion fanfare by blowing out his cheeks and using his feet to kick his desk for a base beat.

On the walls are framed colour prints of smiling dark

faces in bright hats, with painted, shuttered buildings in the background. Ramoul follows my gaze. 'That's my mum and dad. And my kid sister, Cora. And a few aunts and uncles. I've got a big family in Jamaica.' He motions at two seats to the side of a treatment couch.

'You must miss them,' says Mum.

'I've got a lot of family here too, so I'm lucky,' he explains. 'Lived in England since I was ten. Still miss that big hot sun, though.'

'Can you limbo dance?' I ask. Mum raises her eyes to the ceiling in exasperation.

'Are the Black Snakes the best rap group in the world?' he answers.

I take that as a 'yes'.

'They're not,' he whispers. 'The Mother Beepers are. My brother's in the band, so I have to say that.'

'Haven't heard of the Mother Beepers,' I say.

'It's not their real name. But between you and me, the other word is too rude, but I can lend you a CD as long as you wear headphones.' He winks at me and flashes a wide, disarming smile at my mum, who is shuffling slightly in her seat.

'So let's talk the talk. Then we'll take a look at that leg and get to work.'

~

I'm lying on the treatment couch, my nose down a hole. Ramoul is moving my muscles and manipulating my joints, and it's like he's mixing discs on a turntable, blending one movement into another, agile fingers dextrously working the sinews of my body, totally controlled, tuning in to the weak points and stressed areas, easing them back into harmony. I've had loads of massages before, but none have been like this.

'Your back's strong, Amy. You must be some sort of athlete,' he states, working his fingers down my spine to restore some balance after months of uneven walking.

'Let me guess. Kick-boxer?'

'Yeah, right.'

'Pole-vaulter?'

'Nah.'

'I got it. Gymnast.'

'Miles off.'

'These shoulders are the clue. Swimmer, right? '

'Past tense.'

'No ordinary swimmer. Uh-huh. I'd put money on it.'

'County champion freestyle.'

'Holy Horatio, you kiddin' me?'

'Nope.'

'We've just found your gift.' Ramoul is holding out his hand for me to grip with my own.

'What gift?'

'You're going to get back in the water, Amy.' My mum's jaw has dropped slightly. 'Yeah. Because this is Ramoul's Kingdom, where all dreams come true…'

'I can't...' I begin, faltering.

'No such word. That's what my granny says. And if you saw her, you would not, repeat not, argue with her. Man, she has eyes the size of saucers.' He helps me sit up and demonstrates a demon glare, before making more drum noises with his mouth and banging out a rhythm on the couch with his hands.

'"Trouble with yoof, there's too many choices. We wanna be strong, but we hear all these voices. End up just lying around in the grass, when we wanna be loud and sister, kick arse."' Ramoul winks at my mum. 'From the Mother Beepers first, and only, album. Are you getting me?' he asks me, making radio-tuning noises as he pretends to twiddle with my ears.

'Loud and clear.' I'm giving him evil looks. 'And the answer's no.'

~

From:	rabidralph@hotmail.com
To:	amycurtis@ntlworld.com
Subject:	Sound of silence

Lamey,

Howzit goin'? Am worried your silence is due to the fact you have joined an Order of Silent Nuns in Brighton. Are you OK?

Harry x

Poppikins,

Yes, have joined the nuns, but am allowed to sing 'The Hills are Alive' once a month on top of Devil's Dyke (big hill). Have started physio with a total madman with dreadlocks (and bad taste in rap music) called Ramoul. Everything's aching. He wants me to swim again — totally sprocky idea. Need joke, urgently.

Lamey x

25

'What you have to understand, Amy, is that Ramoul doesn't take no for an answer. You with me?' He beams a broad white-teeth smile at me.

We're standing on the beach, watching about fifty people taking off their clothes. There's a stiff breeze and the sea is choppy with white horses steeplechasing over one another.

'You've brought me here to watch a bunch of nutters catch hypothermia?' I ask.

'Uh-huh,' Ramoul answers, pulling his fur lined jacket up round his ears.

'They're not serious,' I say, between clenched teeth.

'Bet your sweet smile they are.' He nods.

The competitors come in all shapes and sizes, from wrinkly oldies to enthusiastic youngies. There's a lot of laughter as they leave their clothes in piles and stride down towards the surf.

'Every year they do this,' Ramoul explains. 'Some of them do it for charity. Some of them do it just for fun. Some of them have their own reasons…' he adds, with a faraway gaze, trying to add an air of mystery.

'It might just be that they're insane,' I suggest, my teeth chattering.

By now they're in and swimming to the starting point by the Brighton Pier. Someone on the shore is holding up a yellow flag. After a few minutes, when they're all assembled in a rough line, the flag is lowered and the race begins.

Supporters on the beach yell encouragement. One carrot-haired kid in front of me turns to us and says proudly, 'That's my granddad.'

'Go, Granddad!' shouts Ramoul.

I stare at him with narrowed eyes. 'Why are we here?' I probe, by now deeply suspicious.

He shrugs. 'You like swimming.'

'Past tense. I keep telling you…'

'It's no good sitting in your chair playing email tennis all day,' he growls. 'Your muscles need to work, like your brain.'

'You sound like my mum,' I mutter.

The swimmers are about halfway to their destination – the derelict West Pier. The strong athletes are creating a lead now. Some of the wrinklies are being left way behind, buffeted by the swelling tide. A lifeguard is keeping a close watch from the shore with a pair of binoculars. Onlookers line the side of the first pier. The police helicopter flies in a circle above the race, before heading east towards the white cliffs of Beachy Head.

'Come on,' orders Ramoul, taking my arm.

'Now what?' I snap at him.

'You want to see the end of the race, don't you?'

'We won't catch them up,' I hiss at him, exasperated, my crutches sinking into the shifting shingle.

'Wrong again.' He grins, opening his rucksack and producing two folded metal scooters, which he proceeds to unfold and lock into shape. He beckons me with his finger, moving off the beach and back onto the concrete esplanade. I try and catch up. It's like walking on peanut brittle. Every shifting step makes a cracking sound.

'You must stand on your right leg and let your left do the pushing.' He demonstrates.

I give him my crutches to hold and attempt to follow his instructions. It feels so strange, my weight on my false leg, but I am moving, even if it isn't in a straight line.

Ramoul overtakes me, my crutches sticking out of the rucksack on his back. 'That's good,' he calls, his dreadlocks blowing in the wind. 'We can dance, if you like.' He rides a figure of eight round me, letting his leg trail behind him.

It takes about four minutes to reach the West Pier. The first swimmers are approaching the finishing flag.

'Hold my arm' says Ramoul, scooping up the scooters and taking my weight.

We move carefully down the shingle and find a good vantage point. Three swimmers are sharing the lead. The carrot kid is jumping up and down by the edge of the surf, waving his arms like a loony. He must have run all the way to get here. He's clutching a blue towel in one hand.

'Come on, Granddad!' he's shouting.

Someone in a yellow swimming hat has taken the lead. A family to the side of us is yelling, 'Go on, Ned – GO ON!'

'Go Ned, my man!' shouts Ramoul and I'm just giving him this 'Shut up, you're embarrassing' look when the family turns round and screams in unison.

'Ramoul – glad you could make it!' enthuses a small woman with grey hair.

'Thanks for inviting me, Angie,' he replies, giving her a big hug, which lifts her off her feet.

At that moment, Ned crosses the flag line and there's a huge cheer from the crowd on the beach. Ned's family hug each other, and then hug Ramoul. They even hug me.

'How do you know them?' I ask.

'You'll see, be patient,' replies Ramoul, wagging a finger at me. The answer to my question follows shortly, as walking up the beach towards us is Ned, an athletic-looking guy of about nineteen, shrouded in a towel. It takes me several moments to realise that Ned is missing his right arm below the elbow. His mum, Angie, takes his prosthetic arm out of a sports bag and Ned fixes it back on before slipping on a T-shirt and jeans. After a few minutes with his family, Ned walks over to us and shakes Ramoul's hand.

'Ramoul. The main man!' says Ned, affectionately, giving him a high-five.

'Hey, big boy. Looking good out there. Brought someone special to meet you. A swimmer,' says my physio, stressing the syllables of the word. I'm shaking my head in disagreement.

Ned looks from Ramoul to me and his face broadens into a grin. 'This guy can be very persuasive,' says Ned. 'Watch out, or you could end up like me, doing triathlons. I'm Ned, by the way.'

'Amy Curtis,' I say. 'That was a brilliant swim.'

'A bit slower than last year, I think.' Ned shrugs. 'There was quite a current out there today.'

'What's your story, Amy?' asks Ned, as he puts on his sweatshirt with 'Chicago Marathon 2004' on the back of it.

'Traffic accident,' is all I can muster, in awe of this athlete.

'Same here. You've heard that story about getting run over by a bus? I was that guy.' He grins. I'm not sure if he's joking. 'I was in the youth squad for shot put and javelin before that. Afterwards, I gave up on everything – became a professional couch potato. Ramoul here had other plans... Anyway, Ramoul, let's catch up. Good to meet you, Amy.'

He shakes my hand, slaps Ramoul on the back and returns to his family, who have organised a flask of hot soup.

'I know what you're trying to do,' I say to Ramoul, between clenched teeth, which are trying not to chatter with the cold.

'I think,' replies Ramoul, narrowing his eyes, 'that you've seen right through my cunning plan,' and before I can hit his leg hard with my crutch, he's running back to the esplanade, laughing like a lunatic.

'The answer's still no!' I shout after him.

'Holy Horatio, these seagulls, so much ugly squawking…' he shouts back, his hands covering his ears.

~

So now we're in the fish and chip restaurant on Brighton Pier, drinking hot chocolate and eating scorching hot fries covered in tomato sauce, looking at the increasingly wild sea through salt-flecked, steam-frosted windows.

'If I'm out of order, I'm sorry,' says Ramoul. He has squirty cream all along his top lip, like a white rabbit's foot. 'I'm not talking about competing again. Just exercising. It's what your body's used to, Amy.'

I bite the top off a chip violently. Sauce bleeds from the wound in big drips.

'You're not saying anything,' he presses.

'I said no.'

'That was because you were cold and grumpy. Man, were you grumpy. And what does Ramoul do? He takes you out for chips. And maybe on to the Häagen-Dazs café, that's how nice I am.'

'It'll take more than triple-chocolate chunks to make me change my mind,' I tell him. I'm hardly going to give up my principles for an ice cream.

He takes a folded press cutting from his pocket, flattens it carefully and puts it in front of me. 'Maybe this'll help,' he says.

I read the headline. 'Swimmer who lost a leg takes on all comers again'. Underneath is a photo of a young woman, standing by an ocean, wearing her swimsuit and goggles. She is very athletic and strong. You don't immediately notice that she is missing her left leg below the knee. I read the caption just underneath. 'Natasha King, a South African swimmer, who made history at the Commonwealth Games in Manchester when she became the first person to compete in both able-bodied and disabled events, is making sporting headlines again, this time at the World Championships…'

'And she was South Africa's most successful medallist at the Paralympics in Athens,' adds Ramoul. 'Five golds and a silver medal. Not bad.'

'How did she lose her leg?' I ask him.

'Motorbike accident. She ranked number two in the country before that.' He reaches for the press cutting and is about to fold it up again.

'Mind if I borrow it, just until our next session?' I say.

'No problem.' Ramoul shrugs. 'I've got a lot of other cuttings in a file in my office. You can look through it sometime.' He gives me a wide grin. 'They're under "I", for "In-spir-a-tion".'

26

'That life is in the past, Ellen.' Dad's speaking very quietly.

Ramoul's reasoned argument, given to Mum at the rehab centre today, is very persuasive, but it's cutting no ice with Dad. Mum's being the mediator, trying to put both points of view. I'm sitting between the two of them at the kitchen table, while my fate is being discussed.

'What does Amy think?' asks Mum, trying to bring me into the conversation.

'Amy is only thirteen,' interrupts my dad. 'She's not old enough to know what she wants yet. I don't want Ramoul filling her head with dreams. She has enough to cope with being disabled. We all have enough to cope with…'

'He's not suggesting she swims every day. Maybe once a week to start with. It would be the best exercise for her, Dave.'

'We moved from Nottingham so she could start a new life,' Dad continues. 'My daughter isn't going to have to suffer other kids pointing and staring at her in the pool.'

I want to say, 'I don't care about that, Dad,' but it's as if I'm not there.

'She needs this to help her walking,' states Mum, trying to keep her temper.

Hello, I'm over here. Whenever I say 'she' in front of

Mum, she always says 'Who's *she*, the cat's mother?' And now, here she is, making out I'm invisible.

'Swimming will make her muscles strong,' she continues.

'There's no future for a disabled swimmer. She would be living with constant disappointment,' counters Dad.

I suddenly look at him in a new light. No one has mentioned competing. Is it just about medals and glory?

'Dad, this is about exercise, not championships. Are you saying I shouldn't have a goal anymore?' I feel proud of myself. That sounded quite mature.

'I'm saying you have to keep your goals realistic,' he answers. 'It's not a good time to be taking on more commitments. Mum's going to be teaching again soon. I don't know what's happening with the contracts or where I'll be...'

This is the first I've heard about Mum going back to teaching. I look at her, surprised.

'It's only going to be part-time, Amy. I can still take you to the pool if you want to go,' she says, gently.

Dad's being so random and bossy about all this – it's not like him at all. I want to wave a magic wand and have the old version back, even though his jokes were terrible.

'And even if, one day, she wants to compete again, it's possible,' continues Mum. 'Loads of people without legs swam in the Paralympics. Show him, Amy.'

I feel in my pocket for the press cutting Ramoul gave me. It's a little crumpled, so I smooth it out on the table. Dad reads it to himself.

"'You have to take what life gives you and turn it to your advantage,'" I quote Natasha's words. 'Swimming was my life, and is still my life.'

I look at Dad, hopefully. He isn't smiling.

'I don't want to talk about this any more,' says Dad. 'I'm not having you go to the pool and being a laughing stock. We need to go forwards, not backwards, otherwise we might just as well have stayed in Nottingham.'

'Are you embarrassed about me, Dad?' I ask, quietly. My heart is thumping in my chest. The sound seems to fill the room.

His face looks ashen and old, suddenly. And very hurt.

'Is that what you think?' he asks, almost inaudibly. He looks from me to Mum, who seems to be waiting for his answer. He just shakes his head and moves his chair back. He pushes his hands into his pockets, the way he does when he's too wound-up to speak, and leaves the kitchen. I make a move to follow him, but Mum puts her hand on my arm.

'Leave it for now, Amy,' she says. 'Dad's under a lot of pressure – the contract he pitched for fell through today. Being self-employed is a big change for him. It's always risky... I'll try and talk to him later.'

Now I'm panicking. Dad and I have always been allies, always had a special relationship. Suddenly I feel abandoned outside the circle of his love. But I can't agree with him, not this time.

Mum and I both jump as the front door closes with a bang. Dad's gone out for one of his long walks and he hasn't even taken Barker.

I'm beginning to realise that losing a leg is just the beginning of a whole bunch of losses. And that there's someone I really need to talk to right now…

~~~

From: amycurtis@ntlworld.com
To: rabidralph@hotmail.com
Subject: Advice

Harry,

I've decided to try the swimming thing — Ramoul has twisted my arm (and almost everything else!). But Dad's gone weird about it. I don't want to deceive him. What should I do?

Amy x

From: rabidralph@hotmail.com
To: amycurtis@ntlworld.com
Subject: Re: Advice

Lamey,

Forget freestyle. My advice is to join a synchronized swimming team and wear a flower on

your head. The advantage is they swim in circles,
so you should be fine. (This action should also
hypnotise your dad, thus avoiding conflict.)
Harry x

PS Fell off a skateboard two days ago (Mum went
ballistic) and sprained my wrist so am tryping this
with mi tongue.

27

So much for Harry giving me advice.

'At the end of the day, you've got to want this more than anything, Amy,' says Dan's voice in my head. 'Only you can make the decision – and if you do, you have to stick with it, twenty-four seven.' That's what he said to me nearly three years ago, before I started my training programme at the pool. Last time, the decision to go for it had been made with Dad's approval.

It seems such a small thing, really – a few lengths once a week. Mum hasn't been able to talk to him about it. They're not exactly speaking. He seems to spend most of his time in his office upstairs, or out at meetings in London. Mum's sure he'll come round in the end. But for now, if I follow Ramoul's advice, I risk making things worse between Mum and Dad. And losing Dad's trust, support and affection.

I've lost enough already, Soph...

But something inside me started reacting when I read the story about Natasha, an invisible life-force, curled and small, that is gradually unfolding its massive wings.

Something called hope.

Barker, who is lying at my feet, suddenly flips over onto his back, offering me his hairy stomach to pat. His tongue lolls out of the side of his mouth, and his eyes plead with me for some stroking.

'Go on then, mutt.' I tickle his chest. His back left leg makes a scratching motion in the air and his throat gurgles with a deep, gravelly noise, indicating great pleasure.

I notice that part of his tongue is a dark-green and purple colour. There's only one reason for this.

'You've eaten my gel pens, haven't you?' When I look under my bed, there's the evidence – two pieces of pen, severely chewed, with their ink missing. 'Bad dog!' I scold. Barker rolls over and turns his back on me, the end of his tail wagging in double time, guiltily.

He has sparked an idea. I reach up to my shelf for a round tin of pens. From the drawer of my desk, I take a small piece of card. I use two pens, an orange and a pink, to write just eight words.

'Amy's Law. Never give up. GO FOR IT'

There, Soph. Now it's official.

I stick the card to the top of my computer with some Sellotape.

'You got a–a–attitude, you excite me, dude, and I wanna be rude, don't wanna start no feud,' sing the Mother Beepers, at full volume on my iPod.

'Ned wouldn't give in,' I tell Barker. 'And Natasha

wouldn't give in. And Ashley Akers. I expect when he said he was going to run a marathon, everyone thought he'd lost it.'

Barker's big brown eyes just stare back, uncomprehending.

'It might have to be our secret,' I whisper. Barker raises his ears and tilts his head in agreement. I put my swimsuit, towel and goggles into my kit bag and pull the zip closed.

'Are you ready, Amy?' Mum yells up the stairs.

'Yeah-s,' I call back. All this fuss for a school interview. I am returning to formal education, after the February half term. Ramoul thinks it's the right time. Now I'm coping with Arthur – the new name for my leg. Half-a-leg. Cool joke, although not one of Ramoul's best...

As I come downstairs, I see Mum dragging on a cigarette. She's wearing a navy suit and shiny, high-heeled navy shoes. Her lips are reddish-orange. She doesn't look like Mum at all. She takes in the sports bag under my arm.

'Only if you're sure...' she says.

'I'm sure.' I nod.

First things first. An hour later, I'm signed up, kitted out and have the T-shirt for Prince Regent College – my sister's school. Caz seems to have settled in OK. She had over a hundred texts from boys in her first week. The girls are, apparently, soooo lovely, especially Bonnie, with the horse and the swimming pool. Or maybe the horse was called Bonnie.

Anyway, no one seems to think my false leg will be a problem, as long as I label it in case it turns up in lost property. The head, Mr Perry, is cool. He has bushy black hair and wears a tie with kangaroos on it.

Mum and I are being shown round the buildings by a spotty fifth-former called Kurt, whose blond fringe completely covers his eyes. The whole place was put up in the 1970s, so it's made of concrete and is quite rectangular and ugly. But there are lots of windows, and it feels light and airy inside. The staircases are quite wide, with rails, so I should be able to brace myself against 1,200 kids changing classrooms at the bell.

Goosebumps. I can smell chlorine...

The pool's only twenty-five metres long and quite narrow. We peer through the glass windows, which are covered in condensation, at the empty, murky water. It looks cloudy and uninviting.

'It looks a funny colour,' I venture.

'Caretaker looks after the pool. He's off with stress,' grins Kurt, who obviously fancies himself as a bit of a comedian.

I look at my watch impatiently and realise I'm counting the minutes until our next appointment, at the Queen Victoria pool in town.

Ramoul is waiting for Mum and me in the pool reception

and greets us both with a high-five.

'So are you ready to do this, Horatio?' he asks.

'As I'll ever be,' I answer, aware that my heart is pounding in my chest.

Mum helps me change into my costume, which seems to have shrunk since last summer. It's cutting into my shoulders, but it will have to do for today.

'Wow,' says Mum. 'Not my little Amy any more.' Cringe.

I sweep my unruly hair under my hat and put my goggles on. I then unstrap my leg and give it to Mum so that I can concentrate on my crutches. Ramoul is right. Late morning is a good time to come. There's only one other woman changing in a cubicle along from me.

'Here goes.' I open the door. Nobody screams in horror. I take my first steps in public unwitnessed by a single soul. While Mum sorts out stashing our stuff in the locker, I take a shower.

A little girl of about two stares at my legs and whispers, 'Poor lady,' to her mum, who smiles at me, apologetically.

Ramoul is waiting for me, in long, lime-green trunks, midway up the pool. There are a few people in the lanes, doing front crawl, plus some wrinklies bobbing about having a chat in the free area. Mum has seated herself in the gallery. She's bought a paper, just like she used to, although I know today she won't read a word of it.

Ramoul props my crutches up against the wall and sits

on the edge of the pool with me.

'Nice tattoo,' I say, admiring the serpent that curls over his left shoulder.

'This is Sydney. He's a water snake, and his spirit will guide you in the water,' says Ramoul, his eyes twinkling.

'Yeah. Right,' I reply. Sometimes Ramoul pushes his luck.

I'm staring at the water, at the ripples on its surface, wondering how many times I've looked down into such warm, inviting depths, waiting for the whistle, willing my nerve endings and my muscles to be patient for a few moments more. It's like being reunited with a long-lost friend. I just want to sink into its enveloping mass and reclaim my natural world, in which I feel one hundred per cent at home.

Ramoul is watching me closely. I swear he can see inside my soul sometimes. He takes my left hand in both of his and interlocks his fingers with mine. It feels fantastically safe.

'In Jamaica there's this thing – a sort of surfer's prayer to the elements. We do it every time before riding our boards out,' he tells me.

I give him a quizzical look. This is probably another wind-up.

'Man, those waves at Makka or Guanna Reef can be facety. Like whales tossing seals about for fun. We don't use words, just actions. Like this.' He releases my hand

and stretches his arms out in front of him, palms upwards. Then, he touches his head, his lips and his heart in turn, finally extending his arms again, with his hands in prayer position. 'That's it.' He beams.

'Yeah, but what does it mean?' I'm waiting for the punch line, confirming I've been made a monkey of, as usual.

'I forgot, you don't speak Jamaican.' He fixes me with a deep, meaningful stare. 'It says, I am at one with you, the ocean and the universe. With my intellect, I respect you. With my voice, I salute you. With my heart, I embrace you. I ask, this day, for courage and protection as I enter your realm.'

His eyes are closed. I know that Ramoul is far away, swimming back to his island, waves crashing around his body, carrying him onto the golden beach beyond.

'What do you see?' I ask, quietly.

'Blue sky, blue sea, Blue Mountains, blue-painted houses. Man! You know, even our national tree is blue? The *Lignum vitae*, wood of life.' He sighs, opens his eyes and beams at me. 'And now I see a kid who wants to get back in that blue more than anything in this world, however high those breakers, however bitchin' that surf. You ready, Amy?'

I nod and take a deep breath.

My left leg slips into the water. I stretch my foot and feel the rush of sensation between my toes. My stump rests obediently on the side at a right angle with my body. I pull my goggles down over my eyes.

'Lower yourself in,' says Ramoul, gently. His calm voice is soothing me. I know that with him here, I'll be fine. I lean forward and drop in almost noiselessly, disappearing under the surface. My ears pop with the sudden change in pressure. In a second, my left foot touches the bottom. I let myself rest there for a moment, taking in the familiar blue world surrounding me.

Remember this feeling, always, I tell myself, pushing off from the tiled floor, reaching up to the surface again.

'How does it feel, champ?'

'OK,' I reply. Actually, it feels mega fantastic.'

He passes me a float. 'Try a width with this.'

Within two strokes I'm in trouble. My stump wants to paddle and can't and my left leg's flailing about, pushing me in circles. Harry was right, after all. I might as well put a daisy on my head and be done with it. The harder I try to go in a straight line, the worse it gets. I can feel my face flushing hot with humiliation. I throw the float back at Ramoul in frustration.

'I can't do it,' I shout at him.

'Of course you can't – yet. Your good leg has to relearn how to perform without its partner. It's moving to a new rhythm. Holy Horatio, you are so impatient…' He's rolling his eyes at me. It's the closest I've come to a telling off.

'Hold the side of the pool and float your legs out behind,' he instructs. Reluctantly, I have a go. 'Move your left leg up and down slowly. One, two, one, two. Now let go and use your arms only – front crawl.'

It's a massive effort, pulling my body weight with just my arms. I'm soon breathless, after only two widths.

'Now bring in your left leg,' calls Ramoul, and I'm not sure if it's exhaustion or panic or what, but I'm in a right tangle. My arms can't seem to co-ordinate with my leg. My right leg just seems to hang in the water, in the way.

I put my hands over my face like a little kid and start crying.

'Amy Curtis,' says Ramoul gently, kneeling on the edge, holding out his hand. 'You know what Bob Marley, reggae king, would say to you?'

I shake my head.

'No woman, no cry. No woman, no cry,' sings Ramoul.

I duck under the water to shut this out. When I surface again, he's still on at me.

'And Sydney says you have done enough for one day. And you're the number one champ, you with me?'

Yeah yeah. Number one chump, more like.

I catch a glimpse of Mum, with her hand over her mouth, trying to stifle her emotions. That doesn't do much for my confidence either.

'Who am I?' asks Ramoul.

'What?'

'I said, who am I?'

'You're Ramoul, my control-freak physio,' I say, in between tears.

'OK, I'll give you that. But I'm also the Magic Master, so trust me. There is nothing you cannot do.'

'Uh-huh.'

'The new Wembley Stadium was not built in one day.'

'You mean Rome.'

'Don't get speaky-spokey. And that's Jamaican for "lippy".' He shakes his finger at me. 'Just be here, the same time next week.'

~

Mum and I are silent on the drive home. When I get inside, I go straight to my room to lie down, while Mum quickly puts my wet towel into the washing machine. (We've thrown away my costume at the pool. Mum says she'll buy me another Speedo one if I want to carry on. Is that blackmail?)

I close my eyes and drift into a weird sleep in an underwater world. Sophie's there, wearing a snorkelling mask and her white trainers, and Harry, who has a sunflower on his head. The lower part of his body resembles a merman, all scaly. Barker's there too, with Sydney the water snake in his mouth, and Mr Perry, the headmaster, wearing a tie made of seaweed. They are all swimming round me and I'm in a silver cage, waving, happy to see them.

And then the sharks come. There are four of them, prowling round the perimeter of the cage, pressing into it, making scraping sounds on the metal with the force of their weight. They look like great whites, with massive jaws revealing sets of jagged teeth. I cower in the middle of the cage, which is almost revolving each time they crash into it. They seem very focused, moving in unison. On each attack, one tries to rip some bars apart with its mouth. Some of the metal is buckling and creating a gap.

I'm shouting for help, but my cries only translate into bubbles, which float away to freedom.

The sharks change tack and start ramming the cage from two sides. Each time, I am thrown against the bars, where a hungry predator waits in hope, its open jaws leading to oblivion.

~~~

From:	amycurtis@ntlworld.com
To:	rabidralph@hotmail.com
Subject:	Disaster

Harry,

You were right. It was a dumbarse idea. I swam like a deformed hippo. I'm never doing it again. Only thing to look forward to now is starting school. Not. How are you? Where are you? Need that joke. Now very urgent.

Amy x

28

From: rabidralph@hotmail.com

To: amycurtis@ntlworld.com

Subject: Re: Disaster

Lamey,

There are two nuns driving their car through
Transylvania when suddenly, Count Dracula lands on
the bonnet, snarling at them through the windscreen.
'Quick, show him your cross!' screams one of the
nuns.

The second nun leans out of the window and yells
'Oi! Get OFF the blinking bonnet NOW!'

Hope that cheered you up. Sorry it took a while.
Mercury has been retrograde, so communications get
delayed. Don't know much about physics/motion, but
swimming with one leg sounds unnatural. Give it up
and take up sky-diving instead.

I'm back in Sunflower Ward — my blood's going green
or something. Write to me soon.

Harry

PS Isabella, she say, 'Hegh-lo.'

'Amy? Can we have a chat?' Dad's knocking on my door. He's been buried under piles of work in his office for the last few days and we haven't really talked, which is probably for the best, because he can always tell when I'm covering something up. And I feel dead guilty, even though my pool trauma was a week ago.

Oh God. Has he found out about the swimming? Didn't Mum hide the towel? MUM! Help! I'm not in the mood for a 'you've let me down' end-of-the-world scenario. I've let myself down. That's bad enough.

Dad's sitting on the bed. He's wearing a faded T-shirt with bleach stains on the front and a pair of grey jogging bottoms. Some of his hair is standing up, as if he's had an electric shock. He hasn't shaved. He looks like some of the doorway beggars in Brighton. He has a funny smell. Old Peculiar – his favourite beer. My dad, the alco-pop.

'Your mum and I have been talking,' he says, scratching his ear and looking at his fingernails for signs of – what? Fleas? Headlice? 'And we think you and Caz should have a holiday.'

Phew. Instant visions of sunbeds and tropical palm trees in Barbados.

'I've been offered a short-term design project in Dorset. One of my old clients from Nottingham owns a holiday cottage down there. Lots of beams and open fires – and a games room. Near sandy beaches. Barker can come too. My client's asked me to help with a barn conversion so

I could work and you lot could just hang out over half term. What do you think?'

Instant vision – a storm-swept beach in the West Country. The five of us huddled under a rain-lashed groundsheet.

'Sounds great, Dad,' I say. Normally, I would give him a hug. But these days, there's no squeezing or shrieking. Just plain old hugs, with no extras. So I sit still, watching him. He waits for a moment, then stands up.

'Right,' he says, disappointed. 'That's settled, then.'

The only condition Caz has laid down is that she needs to have her hair highlighted in a salon, a real shop where all the products smell of peaches or kumquats, while we are away.

'Doesn't sound like the holiday of a lifetime, does it?' Caz mopes, when Dad's out of earshot. 'Bonnie's going skiing in Val d'Isère.'

'Bully for Bonnie,' I reply. 'I'm sure Dorset will have its good points.'

'Duh, right. Like shops selling cream teas and tea towels. Hardly the same as après-ski with a fit instructor, is it? What are you doing with those peaches?'

'Lifting them,' I say, quite politely considering the stupidity of the question.

Ramoul's being a right pain over my exercise programme. He's started me on weights and a high-protein diet. (Sorry, Mum, more meat!) We've ordered some equipment over the internet and in the meantime, he's making me use cartons of orange juice and cans of fruit for practice at home.

'You'll look like a sumo wrestler,' scoffs Caz.

'Hardly,' I reply. 'I'm lifting it, not eating the stuff.'

I'm not going to the pool again. I've made up my mind. I expect Ramoul has already thrown in his trunks, realising I am beyond hope. Some people are born to be heroes. I'm not one of them. I'll send him a text as soon as Caz gives me some space.

'Dad doesn't want you to train,' says Caz, stirring it.

'He said he didn't want me to swim,' I correct her. 'This is just fitness. Shouldn't you be texting Marcus, mwah, mwah?' I ask, deflecting the conversation.

'He's doing his Duke of Edinburgh gold award on Dartmoor. They weren't allowed to take their phones,' she replies. 'And they have to sleep rough for two nights.' Caz wrinkles up her nose prettily at the thought of such shower-facility deprivation. 'So,' she persists, 'you're not going to the pool.'

'No,' I say, truthfully.

'What about Amy's Law?' she pushes, making speech mark signs in the air with her fingers, as if it's something set in stone.

'Laws can be broken,' I reply.

Poppikins,

Why is your blood green? (Always knew you were an alien.) Are you OK? When a2e you going home? We've got to go to Dorset at half term. Caz says there's nothing there except fields, cowpats and fudge.

Write to me pleeeeez.

Lamey

29

It's getting light as we stop in the New Forest for a picnic breakfast – cold bacon rolls (marmalade for Mum) and steaming hot chocolate from a flask. Barker is chasing some wild ponies. He disappeared into the mist five minutes ago. All we can hear is a distant echo of his howl.

'He'll get lost and become the hound of the Barkervilles,' says Dad. Ha, ha. Not.

'Didn't you have time to shave?' asks Mum, turning her nose up at Dad's bristly face.

'It's a holiday, sort of,' he answers. 'I thought you liked the Clint Eastwood look.'

'Every day seems to be a holiday,' she mutters, and gets back into the car, slamming the door.

Caz and I exchange glances. 'You are a bit scruffy, Dad,' agrees Caz, bravely. (Being sixteen, she's nearly an adult, so can almost get away with it.) 'You used to wear suits and funky ties and stuff. And your shoes were always shiny.'

'That was before I broke out of my chrysalis and became a—'

'Slug,' ventures Caz, getting into the car.

'You don't need to dress up when you work from home,' Dad says, almost to himself. He kicks the stony road with his foot and thrusts his hands in his baggy jeans pockets. His hot breath swirls up into the morning sky like a speech bubble with a big question mark inside, before dissolving into the dawn.

Poor Dad. Mum says it's his mid-life crisis.

'Look at this lovely landscape,' sighs Mum. 'We're passing the Salisbury Plain and getting into Dorset now.'

'The cows must have strong legs,' I suggest. 'Some of them are almost vertical.' It's a surreal scene – animals clinging onto hillsides. If someone tilted the hill up a little more, they would all slide off. I giggle at the thought.

'What are you laughing at?' scowls Caz.

'Nothing really.'

'Mum, what's she laughing at?'

'I've no idea, but at least someone in this car is happy,' is all Mum offers in answer to that question.

Dad drives too fast through little villages of whitewashed houses with pretty names like 'Jasmine Cottage' and 'Little Farthings'. Barker starts to whine with excitement, sensing we are near the end of the journey. Mum's gripping the edge of her seat, the way she does when frightened, and keeps shooting angry glances at Dad, who pretends not to notice. Every few miles, there's a farm sign pointing up an uneven track. 'Whiteladies Farm', 'Pear Tree Farm', 'Mossy Bottom Farm'... ('I wouldn't want to sit down in that one,' says Dad.)

'It stinks,' complains Caz, holding her nose. 'It

smells like a sewage plant.'

'It's fertiliser,' says Mum. 'Perfectly natural. Erm, wasn't that the sign for Blue Bottle Farm?'

Dad slams on the brakes. Caz's CDs hurtle through the gap and clatter against the dashboard. Barker, who has been standing up, lands in my lap, upside down.

'Dad!' Caz remonstrates.

'Your mother was map-reading,' he says, weakly, reversing and making the engine scream. Mum is silent. Her eyes are closed. I think she's meditating. We turn right into a narrow track and bump along the rutted surface. High hedges either side of the unmade road stop us seeing any kind of view. The track starts to dip quite sharply. Tall, leafless trees lean over it, like skinny shepherds protecting their flock.

'Look. There's a river,' says Caz, staring wide-eyed at the torrent of water crossing the road where it dips in front of us.

'This is when you wish you had a four-wheel drive,' says Dad lightly.

'Or a tank,' I add, unhelpfully.

Mum only utters three words. 'Stop the car.'

Dad does as he's told. Mum gets out and starts walking down towards the white water. We all just stare at her. She's a bit unpredictable these days. After a couple of minutes, she comes back.

'It's about two feet deep. The car won't get through.

There's a small bridge. We can walk from here. OK, Amy?'

'Fine.' I shrug. 'Arthur could do with a stretch.'

'It might be miles,' moans Caz. Mum chooses to ignore her. Dad backs the car up to a place where it can be left safely at the side of the track. We share out the luggage. Barker goes berserk. Within ten seconds, we hear a splosh. He's in the water, swimming downstream.

'Blue Bottle Farm isn't a very nice name,' observes Mum, looking accusingly at Dad.

'They were going to run wine tastings here,' explains Dad, 'but it didn't work out, so they're going to do holiday lets.'

'Hmm,' says Mum.

As it turns out, the farm is only five minutes away, over the stream and up a steep hill. As we tramp up the driveway, me on my crutches and the others dragging suitcases and carrier bags of food – so there are some advantages! – the sun comes out and makes all the dew on the hedgerows twinkle. A cow moos in the distance and a robin hops between the trees, keeping pace with us. Mum keeps talking to it.

'Hello, Mr Robin. How are you today? Have you found lots of berries to eat?'

Dad says it's Mum's mid-life crisis.

'The rural idyll,' he sighs.

'What's an idyll?' I ask.

Caz groans in her teenage 'You don't know anything, duh-brain' voice.

'The best place imaginable,' says Mum, simply.

But that's where Sophie is, I hope. So there must be lots of idylls, depending on your imagination. In Caz's case, this would be Miss Selfridge.

The track becomes smooth and curves into a courtyard. There's an angel fountain in the middle of this, although there isn't any water coming out of the angel's trumpet. Surrounding the courtyard is a two-storey building with a red tiled roof and small, pretty windows.

'It's lovely,' marvels Mum. Dad looks smug all of a sudden.

Inside the farmhouse, it's warm and inviting, with low ceilings and polished floors and baskets of dried flowers that smell of lavender. From the windows at the back, you can see for miles, all the way down to the sea. It makes me want to run all the way to the horizon. Some chance!

The kitchen is huge, with pine cupboards and a dining table and lots of brightly coloured pottery plates and cups.

All four bedrooms have their own bathrooms, and there are latches on the doors and pink fluffy towels on wooden stands. There are sachets of lavender in the drawers and embroidered irises on the sheets and pillows. Mum and Dad have a four-poster bed with white drapes round it. Mum says she feels like a queen.

Even though there's lots of space, Caz and I decide to share a room, so that we can talk at night. Actually, she's just terrified it's haunted, but funnily enough, I'm not scared of ghosts any more.

'Barker's going to sleep in the kitchen, next to the Aga, so that he can dry off completely,' declares Dad.

Mum and I stare at the view. 'It's very inspiring, isn't it?' she says at last. 'The light is so clear here. See how those fields are defined by the hedgerows? There must be at least six different shades of green…'

Mum hasn't painted a single landscape since the accident. In fact, all her art stuff is still packed in boxes in our attic. I slip my arm through hers and give her a big smile. In my mind, I see her standing at her easel again, wearing one of Dad's old shirts, a look of concentrated pleasure on her face. I'm not sure how, but I know one day soon she is going to reclaim her dreams from the roof space, where they are safely in storage, for now.

I must admit there's something magical in the colours of the wide sky, the sea and the land – uninterrupted by towns and people and the usual obstacles that limit your vision. Here, you can see as far as the ocean. Ideas can take shape and fly. And anything is possible…

I'm going to talk to Caz and Dad about buying Mum a sketchbook. It would be a start.

'There's no satellite,' groans Caz, flipping through a limited range of five channels on the TV.

'But look at all the lovely books,' says Dad, indicating the floor-to-ceiling bookcase, jammed with novels and illustrated guides to walking in the area. Caz shuffles the magazines on the low coffee table and groans again.

'*Ramblers Monthly, Pebble-Dashing in Dorset, Cow's Chronicle…*' She raises her eyes to the ceiling.

After we've explored the garden, which is sunken in parts and has tropical trees, due to the mild winter winds blowing up from Africa and Spain, Dad, Caz and Barker leave to try and retrieve our car. Mum and I sit by the log fire, reading books and eating fruitcake. Mum looks really peaceful and happy.

'This might be a good time to give you something,' says Mum, pulling herself out of her comfy armchair. She disappears upstairs for a while and returns with a plastic bag. 'Go on. Open it,' she encourages.

Inside the bag is a black Lycra Speedo swimsuit. It's not just any old swimsuit. It has go-faster stripes and is designed for racing.

'Mum, I—' I start to protest, but she puts her finger to her lips.

'I just thought, while Dad's working, we could pop into the local leisure centre. Oh, and there's something else.' She gives me an envelope with my name on it. There's a hand-drawn picture of someone diving into a giant wave. And there a beach with a coconut tree. I know who this is from. I take the note from inside. The writing resembles palm branches blowing in a gale, the letters uncontrolled and sloping.

Amy,

Sydney is very unhappy you didn t come to the pool. You have never seen anything so pathetic as a depressed water snake Man, I am up to my ears in reptile tears.

He hopes you enjoy your holiday, but he s worried in case you find yourself falling down a ravine into a waterfall or some white water, now that you are disabled and can t swim at all. He doesn t want you drowning so he has some advice for you

Left arm, right arm, double kick left leg and repeat

I told him to mind his own business, because you are a badass kid who has made up her mind she s going to be a loser. Sydney says you know where he is if you want to talk.

Ramoul

What does he mean, I can't swim? Who is he calling a disabled loser? You have to hand it to him. He really knows how to push my buttons.

'What about Dad?' I ask. It was bad enough deceiving him once.

'This isn't about Dad, Amy. It's about you,' Mum replies. 'Dad's working through some things. But he'll be fine. We'll all be fine,' she says, giving me a squeeze.

I wish she sounded more certain.

For dinner, we toast muffins over the fire and eat

boiled eggs out of china holders with cows' faces on, as darkness spreads across the sky in thick, purple brushstrokes, as thick as our conspiracy. Dad and I have soldiers, narrow slices of toast with butter on. Barker steams gently by the flames, his eyes flickering and his lips curling with dog dreams. Dad threw sticks into the stream so that Barker would jump in and indicate how deep it was. He's still damp and smelly even now.

Finally, it's time for bed. All I want to do is hold my present close. As usual, it takes Caz ages to go to sleep – probably because she has to put eight different face creams on. Her breathing sounds regular now. At last, I can take my swimsuit out of its bag under my bed. I curl myself round it protectively. It smells of new fibres, taut with expectation, and stretchy Lycra, conjuring visions of busy changing rooms, electric with adrenaline.

Downstairs, I can hear Mum and Dad talking. Their voices sound tired and flat. Dad is asking Mum if she wants more wine. She must have said no, because I can hear her coming upstairs.

'Ellen?' Dad is in the hallway at the bottom of the stairs. 'Don't you think we should discuss this?'

'I've been trying to talk to you for the past month, Dave,' Mum replies, quietly. 'I'm tired of doing this on my own.'

'What?'

'Holding it all together, while you have the luxury of "adjusting" to the way things are.'

'The accident…' begins Dad.

'The accident happened. You can't change it. You can't be angry about it for ever. Amy deserves better than this from you.' Mum sighs. 'I'm going to bed.'

I hear the latch on their bedroom door close. And after a few moments, the muffled sound of sadness. I think Mum is crying.

There's a knot in my stomach, and I realise I'm holding my breath. I've never known Dad upset Mum like this before. Should I go and give her a hug? Should I tell Dad to make it up with her? If he were a computer, it would be easy. I could just press the 'Return to original settings' key and I'd have my old Dad back.

Soph, I wish I knew how to mend things…

If it wasn't after midnight, I could maybe phone Harry. The night sister would go ballistic, but it would be worth it, just to hear his voice and have him tell me that parents can be pathetic and it's best to ignore their tantrums if possible.

More than anything, I wish Harry could put his arms round me, like he did that day in Gnome Man's Land, and hold me very tight…

30

I'm eating breakfast in the kitchen and the Coco Pops are sounding like footsteps on gravel every time I crunch them. I'm trying not to distract Dad, who is sitting at the other end of the pine table, shaved and fully dressed, poring over plans of the barn conversion, the project he's advising on down here.

Every sound I make in the awkward silence seems magnified. When you try to be quiet with food, you get strangely clumsy. I've hit my teeth with my spoon twice already. And my attempts at delicate swallowing have resulted in disgusting gulps.

Dad has ignored all of this. His mind is lost in joists and angles. He is tapping numbers into his calculator and scratching his ear.

Now I have a dilemma. There is chocolate milk left in my bowl, but eating it will involve several scraping actions with my spoon. There is an alternative though, so...

'Amy!'

'Sorry. I thought it would be less noisy just drinking it,' I apologise to my appalled father and replace the bowl on the table.

'It's all round your mouth,' he states, disapprovingly.

I move my tongue round swiftly, the way Barker does

when he wants to savour the very last morsel of meaty chunks. 'Gone?'

Dad nods and shuffles his papers, ready to put them back into his case.

'You working today?' I venture.

'Site visit,' he answers.

'It's Sunday,' I say.

'I want to get a head start before tomorrow. I'll be back by lunchtime. Maybe we can go to Monkey World,' he replies.

'Mum says we're doing that on Tuesday,' I tell him.

'Whatever.' He shrugs, snapping the metal clasps shut tight.

'Is Mum awake?' I ask.

Dad shrugs again and drains the coffee in his mug. He always takes her a cup of tea at home, whatever time he gets up. There's no sign that that has happened this morning. The tea bags are still in their box covered with cellophane.

It's serious then, this thing between him and Mum.

'Maybe you and Caz could wander down to the village and rent a DVD,' he suggests.

Duh. Great suggestion, Dad.

'See you, then,' he says, giving me a weak smile. No kiss, no hair ruffling, no hot breath on my neck, which makes me squirm and scream.

The oak front door thuds shut, and moments later, I hear the car engine turning over. It starts to accelerate away. Barker gives a huge, disgruntled sigh, as if to register his displeasure at Dad's departure.

'Never mind, mutt,' I console him, scratching his ears. He turns on his back and lets his tongue flop out onto the red quarry tiles.

'Morning, Amy,' says Mum softly from the kitchen doorway. She looks like a pale woodland nymph, swathed in pink silk, hair loose around her shoulders, which are slightly hunched and sad, like a fairy whose wings have been clipped.

I give her the big hug I saved from last night and offer to make the tea. She wanders to the window overlooking the garden and the fields beyond and stares out, blankly.

'Did Dad say when he would be back?' she asks, at last.

'Lunchtime,' I tell her.

'That doesn't give us quite enough time,' says Mum.

'For what?'

Mum just taps her nose. 'We'll drop him at the site tomorrow, so we girls can have the car,' she states. 'How's that tea coming on?'

Dad still isn't back and now it's five o'clock. Mum's really tetchy for two reasons. Firstly, because Dad hasn't rung and his mobile is switched off, and secondly, because Caz and I found a bike in the garage and we rode it, with me sitting on the metal carrier, down to the village to find the DVD shop. Nothing was open except a little store selling wine and postcards. I bought a card for Gus with a cow on it.

Mum is cross that we did 'such an irresponsible thing'. I point out it was too far to walk and the lanes are very quiet. Plus it was fun, but it's probably better not to mention that.

'You didn't even have helmets,' Mum says, under her breath, chopping carrots violently with a knife.

Caz and I exchange glances.

Barker is standing by the front door, wagging his tail. Seconds later, we hear the sound of a car door closing.

Caz and I exchange glances again.

The front door opens and Dad enters. His cheeks are flushed with fresh air. His trousers and shoes are spattered with mud. Mum carries on chopping without looking up. It's like an old Western movie when the gunslinger enters the saloon and everyone holds their breath...

'Hi,' says Dad, sheepishly. 'I got your messages on the way back. It was a dead spot at the site. Sorry.' He takes in the silent scene and slowly removes his shoes as if any quick action will cause Mum to open fire. Mum opens her mouth to say something, then changes her mind. She pushes the carrots into a saucepan and fills it with water noisily. As she puts it on the Aga, the water droplets on the pan make a hissing noise.

Or maybe it's the steam coming out of Mum's ears.

Dad helps himself to a beer from the fridge and pulls

the ring. It makes a satisfying, wet, 'ssshhhing' noise. He drinks from the can, looking at Mum. If this were a movie, she would probably slap his face now, or blow his Stetson away with a sure shot from her rifle.

Instead, she just pulls a cabbage from its plastic bag and puts it on the wooden block.

'There was more to sort out than I thought,' he says. 'I'll leave early tomorrow so we can all do something together.'

'We're having a girls' day out,' Mum informs him. 'I'll drop you at work.'

'Right,' says Dad, a bit taken aback.

'We didn't agree to be marooned here,' she adds tersely, slicing the cabbage sharply and putting it into the saucepan.

'No, of course not,' he agrees. 'I'll, um, go and have a shower. Clean up.'

'OK,' says Mum, who is now wreaking vengeance on a defenceless onion. 'By the way, Mr Bingley phoned earlier.'

Mr Bingley is Dad's work client who offered us this farmhouse for our holiday in return for help with the barn conversion.

'Oh?' says Dad.

'Yes. He wondered why you hadn't been to the site all day,' states Mum, holding Dad's gaze. 'I didn't know what to tell him.'

Caz and I look from Mum to Dad and back again. The cabbage is wilting in boiling water. The bubbling liquid is the only sound in the room.

Dad seems to age before our eyes. His face is heavy with emotion. There are deep shadows under his eyes.

'I just couldn't...' he begins, his hands open, almost pleading with Mum to understand without him having to explain.

'Couldn't what?' she asks, more gently, moving towards him.

'I just walked. All day,' he tells her, before turning to leave the kitchen, his damp socks making patterns on the tiles.

Mum closes the latch door after him and sits down with us. Her hands are clasped. She is concentrating hard on what she is going to say.

'I don't want you to worry about Dad,' she says firmly. 'He's feeling a bit low. Doctors call it depression. A lot of people have it. It makes them retreat into their shells.'

'Is it catching?' asks Caz, helpfully.

'No,' Mum says.

'Can I still get my highlights done tomorrow?' my sister persists.

'Yes,' sighs Mum.

'Dad's going to get better, though,' I state.

Mum nods. 'With our help. He just needs us to carry on as usual. We can manage that, can't we?' she entreats.

"Course,' Caz and I say, in unison. I have visions of Dad, riding off into the sunset alone, leaving us behind at the Not-So-OK Corral...

'So, tomorrow, Caz will have highlights and Amy and I will do a little exploring,' says Mum. 'And life will go on...'

31

I slip into the water almost soundlessly. It wraps itself round me like a gossamer web, supporting my weight. I push off from the side and lie on my back, floating, looking at the black ceiling and its universe of twinkling stars. I can hear the sound of my heartbeat in my ears, which are just below the water – my rhythm, loud and clear.

I start to pull my arms back, one, two, one, two, letting my legs trail in the pool. After all the weightlifting, my muscles are strong and capable. I reach the end of a length in no time. Next I'll try front crawl, again without my legs.

I kick off from the side, put my face flat in the water and start to reach arm over shoulder, breathing on every third stroke. Here goes, Ramoul. Left arm, right arm, double kick left leg and repeat. Holy Horatio, it's working! And it feels great, moving fast and smoothly across the surface.

When I approach the end of the pool, I prepare to do a tumble-turn. I have to remember to kick off with my left leg. I just have to concentrate...

Brain, why are you somersaulting, bombarding me with images from the past, replaying my experiences in fast forward?

I'm five and I'm about to do my first underwater flip. There's water up my nose and in my eyes – my goggles are a bit big, but they were the last pink pair and Dad gave in... I can see the tiles at the end of the pool, and soon I've got to scrunch up like a sleeping cat and roll my body over...

Three strokes more – one, two, three and CURL! I hear Dan's voice in my head, strong and insistent. I turn underwater and make myself resist my habit of drawing my right leg back ready to power off the wall. Do it, my brain tells my left leg and it responds. Ouch! I've scraped my toes on the tiles, because the angle isn't quite right.

But I'm up and moving again. The rhythm is working well – the double kick is feeling more natural now.

Ten lengths! I'm into my stride. I start breathing every six strokes. My chest feels fine. My arms are great. My legs are tired but coping. The only things that hurt are my eyes, because I haven't got my goggles.

I'm swimming blind. I'm eight and it's my first out-of-county competition. Caz thought she was being clever, hiding my goggles in her room, and there wasn't time to find them before leaving. Dad and I got caught up in motorway traffic and I've missed the warm-up, but it doesn't matter because I'm so fired up, my body's jet-propelled, eating up the distance. I'm leading by at least a metre and ahead of me is just beautiful, empty blue...

Twenty lengths and my arms are beginning to complain a bit. It's OK, I reassure them. Just relax and go with the flow.

Thirty lengths. Now my mind's going into positive neutral, the place it always used to settle when I was training.

I can feel adrenaline rushing through my whole body. Ten lengths more and my fingers are touching the side. I want to let out a scream of joy.

'That's a thousand metres without stopping,' calls Mum, who is watching me from the stands. Judging by the clock on the wall, it has only taken me twenty minutes. That's not bad for a kid without a kicking leg.

I'm eleven, swimming lengths with my club, working on lengthening my strokes and Dan's timing me with his stopwatch and talking to my dad, who is nodding. And Dan's motioning for me to stop and he's bending down to show me the time on the display. It's a whole four seconds faster than my personal-best time for 100-metres freestyle. Dan is telling me how impressed he is, how he thinks that, with training, I could go all the way...

There's clapping from the other side of the pool. When I look round, the lifeguard who is seated on top of the raised platform gives me the thumbs-up.

I pull myself out of the water, which has built up quite a swell with my performance, splashing over the edge of the tiles. I watch it quieten into stillness once more. Mum comes down from the stand to help me. As she does so, the women enjoying a water-aerobics class give me an ovation with their feet!

I'm elated and STARVING! Mum says we can have smoothies in town when we pick Caz up from the hairdresser's.

'Amy, what's wrong?' she asks, as my knees buckle and I grab her arm to stabilise myself.

'When you said "smoothies", everything went out of focus, Mum.' It takes me a minute to compose myself.

'Maybe it's your blood sugar. That was a big effort,' consoles Mum, her eyebrows furrowed with concern.

My first secret outing to the pool since that awful nightmare about the sharks.

I can feel my fitness, and my confidence, starting to grow. Mum has been mega fantastic. She's totally on my side. She's even bribing Caz with a series of beauty treats so my sister doesn't squeal.

'I told Dad we were going to explore the lanes, which is technically true,' says Mum. 'When the time's right, we'll tell him together, OK?'

'I want to tell him, Mum. And soon,' I answer, sounding as if I have thought it through, which couldn't be further from the truth. I'm just delaying the dreadful moment. I start to sing the chorus from the lead track on the Mother Beepers' one and only album. 'Just take control, you know you want to, you know you want to.'

'Amy...' Mum is staring at me with her mouth open.

I realise I am walking towards the car, carrying my crutches in my left hand.

Mum and I give each other a massive hug. It goes on for about a minute, and it's so hard it's squeezing tears out of our eyes. We're both laughing like lunatics. Anyone watching will think we've been let out of a nuthouse.

The clown has gone for good, Harry…

On the journey into town, Mum keeps beaming at me. I'm hoping Caz has had time to organise the special surprise for her, because she's been brilliant. Mega Mum.

It's a short walk from the car park to the High Street, and when we approach the salon where we dropped Caz this morning, I see that my sister is already waiting outside – her layered and golden-tinted hair gleaming with products and attracting admiring glances from passers-by. She is holding a crisp, white bag with 'Arnold's Stationers' and Art Supplies' on the front.

'We'd like to give you this now,' Caz and I say to Mum. 'It's from all of us.' That's not strictly true as we haven't had a chance to discuss it with Dad, but I'm sure he would agree it's a great idea.

'Thanks for everything, Mum,' I say. She opens the bag and takes out a large sketchbook and a box of artist's pencils. Her hand goes to her mouth. She looks surprised and overcome all at once and says 'thank you' very quietly and gives us both a kiss.

I know that without her, the great leap I've just made might never have happened. Maybe now, her talents can take flight too.

'You must all have been reading my mind…' she says.

As we head towards the tantalising smell of pizzas in a nearby restaurant, I feel surer than ever that we all have our own paths to follow. Thanks to Mum, I'm back in the lanes, after being lost in the wide, open water.

And in my mind, I'm rehearsing my argument. 'This is my life, Dad, and from now on, I'm taking control of it. I have a dream – and there's no reason why it can't come true…'

Cheesy, but not a bad start.

32

We've just arrived back at our house in Brighton and the phone is ringing. I'm hoping it's Ramoul because I've sent him loads of texts and messages on his mobile. I can't wait to tell him the good news. I'm the first one in and I hurry to pick up the receiver.

'Ramoul?' I say, ready to ask him to hang on while I take the phone to my room, out of Dad's earshot.

''lo, Ame.'

'Dollop. Sorry, I thought you were someone else. I'm waiting for a call…'

'Got your postcard. The cow was funny.'

'Thought you'd like it. Look, can I call you back in a little while? We've just got home and we've got all the unpacking to do and stuff…' I can hear him sigh on the end of the line. 'Actually, it's OK. Did you want to tell me something?'

'It's a secret.'

'I promise not to tell, then.'

'Colin's had babies. They're all brown and white, like the cow.' His voice is high-pitched and excited.

'Wow! So Colin's a girl?' I'm imagining Sophie's flat full of guinea pigs, on the sofas, on the dining table, on the kitchen floor, all squeaking in unison…

'What did your mum say?' I ask.

'She said "that's nice". She's taking pills that make her smile all the time. I think she's very happy now,' he explains.

'Can you look after all those guinea pigs?' I say, gently.

''Course,' he sniffs. 'Can you come and see them, Ame? They're very pretty. There's one with a star on its face.'

'I'd like to, Dollop. But it's a long way now. Maybe you could draw them and send me the picture?' This sounds so hollow and I feel really mean saying it.

''K, Ame. Oh,' he says, exasperated, 'got to go. The star one's done it again, all over the floor.'

'Oh no,' I respond, not sure what to say.

'Doesn't matter. What they do – poo all day.'

And with that, he's gone. In the pit of my stomach, I feel really sad and lonely. My connection with Shirley and Gus feels like the strand of a spider's web spun over a huge distance – bending and flexing in the breeze and in danger of breaking…

I said I would be his big sister. Soph, I'm so sorry…

And now the phone's going again. This time it's Ramoul.

'So, give it to me.' It sounds like he's holding his breath.

'Ramoul, I did the fifteen hundred, and I've worked out how to use my leg and you were so right about the rhythm, and the tumble-turns were OK as long as I remembered to kick off with the left and…'

On and on I go, without pausing for breath.

'Hey! Hold the phone – you are giving me serious earache,' he laughs.

'I want to train again, properly, every day,' I hear myself saying.

'Holy Horatio,' Ramoul gasps, totally over the top.

'That's not all. I'll need to join a club. I want to compete.'

A moment's silence. Surely he's not going to say no?

'Anything else, m'lady?'

'I want you to get me really fit. As fit as Natasha King. And I want to do the piers race next year, like Ned.'

'Were you always this bossy?' he asks.

'No.' I smile. 'Meet the new Amy Curtis.'

So, the deed is done. There's no going back. And now I have no choice but to tell Dad. I feel like throwing up. My palms are sweaty, and my tongue has gone dry. I think it has to be now, this minute, before I lose my nerve...

'Dad? Any chance we can go for a drive?' I say, lightly, as he's just about to pull the ring on a can of beer.

'We've just driven a hundred miles, Amy.' he says, looking perplexed.

'I know, it's just I wanted to talk to you about something.'

Dad looks at Mum, who flashes him one of her 'Just do it' expressions, while she chops up Barker's meat and biscuits in his bowl extra manically, her nose averted upwards away from the smell.

'It's dark,' he complains. 'Where do you want to go?'

'Oh, I don't know. The seafront maybe.' I'm hoping the wide expanse of English Channel will swallow the explosion that will inevitably follow my confession.

Dad looks at his beer wistfully and puts it back in the fridge.

Mum mouths, 'Shall I come?' and I shake my head. I don't want her to fight my battles. I'm almost fourteen.

Dad dutifully drives us down to the lower esplanade east of Brighton Pier. We park and watch the hundreds of light bulbs along its length flash on and off like bats' eyes, blinking. The sea is a wide, flat expanse of indigo blue, illuminated by a full, round moon.

'See that big trawler on the skyline?' asks Dad. 'Imagine spending months at sea like those guys do – just catching glimpses of land.'

I can identify with that – being cast adrift from the people you love.

'It was a great feeling out on the water,' Dad continues. 'Dreamed of going solo across the Atlantic when I was your age.'

'You should have asked Santa for a boat for Christmas,' I say, unsure how to respond to this revelation.

'I had a dinghy – *Kestrel*. Well, shared it with your Granddad Will. He helped me get my navigator's exams when I was fifteen. I sailed *Kestrel* round the Isle of Wight at sixteen. Got offered the chance to crew for a British team in the America's Cup. But then Granddad died. We had to sell the boat…'

Dad is staring out to sea, sadly.

'You could buy another one now,' I suggest.

Dad shakes his head. 'When you race, it takes everything out of you. You go away for days, sometimes weeks, for the internationals. Too old now, anyway. And your Mum hates the water, so it would be a bit selfish. Can't imagine Caz wanting to get the wind in her hair. So it would just be you and me…'

That doesn't sound so bad, I'm thinking…

'It's just life. You compromise and file your dreams away for a rainy day,' sighs Dad. 'I didn't become a yachtsman, and Mum didn't take her place at the Slade School of Art in London because of me. She could have been really successful. She was the most talented student on her degree course. That's what she told me, anyway.' He pulls a silly face. Dad the joker is never very far away from Dad the moody, middle-aged person.

'What if you didn't have to keep your dreams locked up?' I blurt out. 'What if you could make them happen?'

'That's not reality, Amy,' replies Dad. 'Dreams come at a cost. Sometimes, the price isn't worth paying. That's why I don't want you wasting your time on trying to turn the clock back. You've got to move on. Sorry if I sound like an old fart full of doom.'

I really don't get it. Dad's not being rational. He's the one who's wrapped up in the past, with a life jacket round his neck. Maybe that's what Mum meant when she said he was 'working through things'. He needs Doctor Who's Tardis to transport him back to the present. I have a sudden vision of him in black, time-traveller gear, and I'm there, at his side, his sparky, sassy helper. And we're being pursued by Daleks down a long, narrow corridor...

'Exterminate,' I say suddenly.

'What?' says Dad, giving me a weird look.

'Nothing, sorry. What were you saying?' Brain, keep on track, this isn't the time to go off one of your mad adventures.

'It's mild depression. Nothing serious. Just gravity pulling my face out of shape,' he says, dropping his jaw onto his chest and pinching at least two inches of jowls either side.

I'm taking this in. Does it mean Dad's going to look like a bloodhound for ever now?

'The important thing is, we've all got each other. So we're OK, aren't we?' says Dad, squeezing my hand. A heaviness has settled round his shoulders like a rain-soaked cagoule.

'Yes, we're OK,' I reply, my heart sinking.

'Now, what was it you wanted to talk to me about?' he asks.

'Um. I've been worried. About you and Mum.' This is the most truthful thing I can come up with in the circumstances. 'You used to buy her flowers on a Friday. And tango with her in the kitchen. And write messages to her in flour on the table... You used to make her laugh.'

Dad nods slowly. 'The human formerly known as

David Curtis has been taken over by a creature from the planet Zarp, which has no known emotion or knowledge of dance steps,' he says, in a strange voice.

'Right,' I say, wishing Dad would stop talking to me as if I'm a little kid.

'The thing with Zarpoids,' continues Dad, sensing my displeasure, 'is they dissolve after a period of time and are absorbed into the bloodstream.'

'Do they leave long-term damage?' I ask.

Dad shrugs. 'No after-effects. Fluorescent poo for a couple of days, in rare cases.'

'So you and Mum…?'

'Tango partners mate for life.' He smiles, patting my hand. 'Like swans.'

'Right,' I say, unconvinced.

'I enjoyed our little chat,' says Dad.

'Me too,' I say, my eyes resting on the black clouds drifting heavily across the moon.

I'm sitting on my bed, holding Soph's silver teddy, trying to breathe in and out very slowly and deeply, the way Dan taught me to do when my nerves needed calming. My pulse is racing, despite this. Half an hour ago, I was braced to tell Dad the thing he wants to hear least in the whole world. That I've deceived him. But the words never left my mouth. They're still prisoners in my mind.

We stopped at Tesco on the way home and Dad bought Mum a big bunch of orange lilies. When he got back in the car, he had pollen on his nose. It looked quite cute so I didn't say anything.

Mum gave me a thumbs-up sign when he wasn't looking, so I shook my head and she sighed a big sigh. She asked why and I just said, 'Ask him about the planet Zarp,' before coming upstairs.

At least Dad and Mum are having a glass of wine downstairs. Hopefully, the acid from the fruit will help the alien creature dissolve a bit more quickly...

Soph, I need to talk to you so much. Adults speak a different language – you have to understand the things they don't say. I want to do that random-babbling thing with you – the one that really annoys parents and makes us crease up. I wish we could just hang out like we used to and you could get your whole weird wardrobe out and ask me to choose what you're going to wear for your next photo shoot...

I've looked up depression on the internet and now I'm feeling depressed.

Dad's got at least half of the symptoms – tiredness and loss of energy, persistent sadness, loss of self-confidence and self-esteem, difficulty concentrating, undue feelings of guilt or worthlessness, sleeping problems (that explains his post-midnight fridge-raiding routine), avoiding other people, sometimes even close friends...

It's happened since the accident Soph. It made us stop being who we were. Except Caz, maybe. She's as sprocky as ever.

There's a single knock on my door and my sister is entering my room, looking like an extra from a Goth movie, with long, black streaks down her cheeks and red eye-pencil outlining her bloodshot eyes. She's wearing her old pink dressing gown over her jeans and T-shirt – the one with the rabbit embroidered on the pocket. She isn't meeting my gaze. Instead, she slumps heavily down on my bed, her face buried in my duvet.

'What's up?' I ask. She reaches inside her rabbit pocket and produces her mobile phone.

'Read it,' she instructs. I scrutinise the text display panel. It says, 'Soz but time 2 say bye. Marcus xxx'.

Caz is crying now, in long, painful gasps. 'He (sob) slept with Rachel Turner (sob) in her tent because she had hypothermia (sob sob). And she's got braces (gulp) and eyebrows like Barker (sniff). And don't say (sniff) there are plenty more fish in the sea.'

'I wouldn't. It's not true. Fish will soon be extinct,' I point out.

'Urgh,' she says, giving me a hard push. She notices the silver teddy in my left hand. It's almost reflected in her wide, blue, sparkling, wishing-pool eyes.

'Hearts mend,' I say, and she nods. I don't mention that they never lose their dark chambers, which we seal up tight. The spaces where the light of the people we love once shone…

33

From: rabidralph@hotmail.com

To: amycurtis@ntlworld.com

Subject: Tortoise and the hair

Lamey,

Thanks for the postcard. Mum brought it in today.
You were lucky to go to Monkey World. I've always
wanted to go there. The one with the spiky (air
looks like your sister. Don't tell her I said that.
I've had another op — they said it was a blood clot,
but I know it was the sherbet lemon Nurse Emmerson
gave me, which got stuck in my small intestine. I'm
going to sue McDougals of Fife (who made it) and buy
a Porsche on eBay. I'm doing OK now.

Have got masses of work from the tutor my school's
sent. He looks like a tortoise. I've told him I'm
self-educating — up to U in the mobile library now.
Ask me anything you like about Uzbekistan!

Congrats on the amazing u-know-what in Dorset. You
have defied physics and are a human miracle. Catch
ya later.

H x

PS Bald is no longer the new black, so am growing
my hair again.

From: amycurtis@ntlworld.com
To: rabidralph@hotmail.com
Subject: Thanks

Poppikins,

Not another operation!!?? You'll qualify for *The
Guinness Book of Records* if you're not careful! Glad
u r OK now. Still haven't told my dad the dark
secret. He's got depression and is acting a bit
weird, so it's probably not a good time. What
colour is your hair? What will happen to Ralph?
Thanks for admitting I'm a human miracle — at last.
You can't ignore the truth for ever!

First day of school tomorrow. Wish me luck.

Lamey x

I look stupid in my grey uniform, like a lamp post. The
trousers are slightly too big and they hang on my narrow
hips. The arms of the jacket are a bit long. (Mum meant
to sew them up but hasn't got round to it.) I still haven't
had my hair cut, so I've scraped it up into a pony, but that
still leaves my fringe flopping halfway down my face.

Caz says I should have 'hair assessment' and 'follicle
analysis', like she did in Dorset. I remind her that for two

hours, she looked like a squirrel with its fur flicked out. Until our trip to Monkey World, where it rained and her new hair clung to her head like cling film.

'Ooh-hoo, ooh-hoo, ooh-hoo,' said the monkeys, when they saw her.

Anyway. School. Standing in the hallway waiting for Mum to find the car keys, I experience some strange medical symptoms, all within the space of five minutes. The first is the desire to throw up, which might have been to do with the porridge Dad cooked with water instead of milk. The oats clustered together in the pan, forming hard, round lumps similar to meatballs. I can feel them progressing down to my stomach.

The second sensation is dizziness – the kind when your eyes blur over and your palms go sweaty. I sit on the stairs and put my head between my knees. Barker thinks I'm playing a game and tries to seek me out with his hard, wet nose.

The third sensation, which becomes the dominant one during the car journey, is that of a thousand butterflies dancing in my tummy. I expect them to come pouring out of my mouth when I open it to speak. So I keep it zipped shut, just in case.

When we get to the gates, I want to tell Mum to take me home again, and she looks like she wants to. But Caz is grabbing my bag and opening my door and before I know it, I'm walking, without my crutches, up the black tarmac driveway. I probably look a bit like a Munster from the back, because when I turn to wave, I see Mum's face buried in a tissue.

And right at this moment, the butterflies turn into fire-breathing bats, flitting about in my internal organs, scorching everything in sight and emitting an ear-piercing squeal.

Caz is really patient and waits for me to get to the reception, where she hands me over to the secretary, Mrs Rhodes, an efficient-looking woman with a bun, a purple suit and pink lipstick.

'Hello Amy. Welcome to the College.' She smiles. 'This is Georgia and she is going to be your shepherd today.' She motions to a short, pretty girl of about fourteen, who has her hair tied back with lots of plaits.

'Hi,' says Georgia. 'You've got to put up with me today.' She gives me a little wave and a big grin. I notice she is wearing several strings of woven bracelets on her wrist, in rainbow colours.

Maybe today isn't going to be the second worst day of my life after all.

'We're on the first floor,' explains my new companion, apologetically.

'No problem.' I shrug and start to follow her. A stream of lamp post kids jostles past us, going up and down the flights of stairs. I hold on to the rail and make good progress.

'You get used to the crowds,' says Georgia. 'I came here from a village school – there were only fifty of us in total. There are forty kids in a class here, so I was completely out of my depth and I hid in the loos for a whole morning.'

'How long did it take you to find your way round?' I ask, wondering if I'll ever get my bearings in this huge place.

'A couple of days. But you'll be fine. I won't let you out of my sight.' She gives me another big grin.

The noise and energy everywhere help carry me forward. The great thing is that no one is staring at my leg. Everyone seems focused on getting to where they need to be.

We reach the classroom, a rectangular space with a continuous line of big windows down one side, from which you can see the sea in the distance. Georgia takes me to a desk with two seats near the front.

'We're sitting here,' she says. 'There's a locker in the corridor for your books and coat and stuff. Nice view, isn't it?'

'Yes,' I reply. Something strange passes up my spine – a memory of a different view, over chimneys and fields, rivers and forests to the Pennines beyond, which, when I blink, is still more real than this moment. And it is Sophie who is sitting next to me, with her fluffy pig pencil case and her ruler with teddies on it, winding her blonde hair around her finger. And she's yawning and putting her head on my shoulder and asking me to wake her up when double maths is finished.

'Amy Curtis?' I hear my name. There is a man with round, blinking eyes standing at the front of the class. 'I'm Mr Norvill. Welcome to Form Two. Do you have your weekly schedule?'

'Yes,' I reply, fumbling for my information pack in my rucksack. I show it to him. He claps his hands together, a little like a squirrel.

'Excellent. Any problems, come to me.' Blink blink.

By now, the twenty tables in the room are nearly full. There are more girls than boys. Everyone so far has said hello. Mr Norvill introduces me officially before calling the register. On the way to assembly, Georgia shows me where the loos are in case I feel like hiding.

It's weird, being a schoolkid again. I'm just one of the crowd here. For the last six and a half months, I've been someone with special needs, suspended in time, surrounded by adults – apart from my stay on Sunflower Ward – and cocooned. It's fantastic to be around friends gossiping and laughing. And it's brilliant to feel part of a group that is accepting me as I am, not remembering how I used to be.

In assembly, I gaze around the massive hall at the hundreds of kids standing in lines. The sixth-formers have chairs in front of the stage, and above them sit the staff, about sixty teachers, some of them in gowns and mortar boards. Everyone has to stand when Mr Perry comes in, except the musicians in the orchestra, who are ready to play near the grand piano.

'Good morning, everyone. We'll begin with hymn number seventy-four – "Glad that I live am I".'

Oh Soph, why did it have to be that one?

The music begins, and, next to me, Sophie is clearing her throat, ready to sing her special version of the song, and a few rows behind us, Hot Stuff and his mates are dropping their hymn books, being pathetic, and my mind is on the training that I did that morning, pleased that I managed to shave a tenth of a second off my 200-metre personal-best time...

'Glad that I live am I, that the sky is blue. Glad that I have one eye, so I can't see you...'

But a few seconds and a single action, like a bolt of lightning hitting the earth, has changed all that and now I'm transported to a new place, mentally and physically, standing with strangers, living two realities, rerunning the reel of my life.

I feel like I've been here before. The music is the same – it's just me who has changed.

My throat is tight and I'm having to mime the words. Georgia glances at me and crosses her eyes to show she is bored. Soph always did that, always knew how to cheer me up. And suddenly, my voice breaks free. I'm singing and the words have a new meaning.

'Glad that I live am I...' *I am the lucky one and I'll never forget it, Soph.*

The first lesson is double English and the teacher, Mrs East, asks the class to tell me the plot of *Animal Farm*, a novel by George Orwell which they have all been studying. I quickly suss out the introverts from the extroverts.

'Four legs good, two legs bad,' everyone chants in unison, making assorted pig noises. I get to judge the best summary and have to give my reasons. Then the winner gets a chocolate bar and Mrs East gives me a copy of the book to read by next week. I think English is my favourite subject now.

At breaktime, Georgia takes me to the refectory, where you can buy snacks and drinks and where we have lunch every day. There are loads of long tables, so you can sit with your mates. I meet Georgia's friends Ally, Rachel and Debs, who are in other classes. We're chatting away about everything – pop groups, boys, TV, films, like we've known each other for ages. They're really easy to talk to.

'We're going to see *Teen Queen* on Saturday. Would you like to come?' asks Rachel, and I feel a rush of excitement at the prospect of going out in a group, without parents, sisters or a secret kit bag in sight.

'That would be great,' I say. 'Thanks.' I can't wait to

tell Mum. She'll be dead chuffed. I've only been here a few hours and I've already got ten MSN addresses for some online chatting tonight...

It turns out Georgia likes swimming too – and she's got a dog – so we've got loads in common. I tell her about Ramoul and my attempts to get my speed back up in the water.

'It's brilliant that you're training again,' she says, impressed.

'Except that I haven't told my dad,' I confide, as we're making our way to double science. 'He wants to wrap me up in cotton wool and protect me from the world.'

'It's a dad thing,' she says, simply. 'They can be very annoying.'

'And embarrassing,' I add.

'Definitely!' We both laugh. Georgia links her arm through mine, as if we've been friends for ever. I feel safe and secure. And happy.

'So far, so good?' she asks.

'Mega-tastic,' I reply. 'Can't believe I've just said that about school!'

Finally, I'm putting books away in my locker and it's the end of the day. There are voices all round me and surges of bodies moving in every direction, like currents of water converging. My back is aching from all the walking, but I feel light and energised from all the different stimuli. I've got a few months' work to catch up on, but all the teachers have said they'll give me extra help if I need it.

'Bye, Amy,' says Georgia and gives me a hug. 'Oh. I've got something for you.' She takes one of her bracelets off her wrist, the one woven with pink and blue threads, and gives it to me. 'There,' she says, securing it on my arm. 'We're proper friends now. See you later, alligator…'

Suddenly, I feel a bit faint and have to hold on to the locker door. Things are moving round and round. I'm spinning in the front garden with Sophie, I'm tumbling under the water and reaching for the surface, I'm rolling around on the floor of our old house with Dad, screaming with laughter and I'm drifting, in my dark place, towards oblivion. The images merge and fade. My eyes are closed and yet I am still moving. Everything is silent, except the beating of my heart.

'Are you OK?' Georgia is asking. Her voice is an echo, getting louder. Slowly, the motion inside my head subsides. I open my eyes. My forehead is hot and the inside of my mouth has gone completely dry.

'I'm fine,' I say and manage a smile.

I don't really feel fine, though. I'm like a lizard that is shedding its skin too early. I'm leaving my old life behind – or it's leaving me. I didn't expect to feel this way. You get so used to being sad that it seems normal. People around you use words like 'adjusting' and 'compromising' and 'accepting'. You believe your life is always going to be less than it was.

Yet today, I've experienced something amazing. I've got new friends, things happening. I've had a good time – lots of laughs. I've even forgotten about my leg for a few precious minutes. I've been Amy and it's great to be back.

I expect you think I'm shallow and selfish and disloyal, Soph. Maybe I am. I still miss you so much it hurts. No one will ever take your place. But I'm tired of the pain. It's like a heavy coat wrapped round me – a straitjacket. I nearly came with you, but something stopped me. So I've got another chance with my life and I want to go for it. Amy's Law, right? I'm starting to look forward. I'm starting to breathe again. I don't want to feel guilty anymore. I hope all this makes sense and that you don't think I'm the most horrible person in the history of time.

I'll always love you, Soph.

34

Mum's driving me down to the pool. Luckily, Dad's away working in London, so we don't need to cover our tracks. It's seven o'clock. I haven't stopped talking since she picked me up from school.

'You found it all right going up and down stairs?' Mum keeps probing.

'Fine,' I reply. 'So, anyway, is it OK for me to go to the cinema on Saturday?'

Mum pulls into a space at the pool and switches off the engine. She takes her seat belt off and gives me a hug. I'm expecting the inquisition, a list of questions about who, what, why, where and when.

'Of course,' she replies simply. Result!

By keeping Arthur on, I'm in and out of the changing room in only ten minutes this time and by the poolside within twelve, with my hat and goggles in place.

We've booked a lane for half an hour so that I can train and then I've got my weekly aqua physio with Ramoul. The thought of easing into the warm water has kept me going all through my nerve-wracking, but surprisingly great, day. Mum settles herself in the gallery with her paper. She waves at me and gives me a cheery smile, followed by a thumbs-up.

I can see the freckly lifeguard staring at me intently, as I walk carefully towards the deep end. The next part is tricky – removing Arthur and propping him up against the wall, whilst not falling over and embarrassing myself. Any moment, I expect the whistle to sound and for a voice to shout, 'You can't leave that monstrosity there,' but no sound comes, so I sit and shuffle on my bottom to the edge of the pool.

But what I really want to do is dive.

If I could just kneel up and balance on my hands, I would be able to stand on my left leg. It's worth a try. I wobble and sway my way into an upright position and concentrate on steadying my posture, before bringing my arms up over my head into a torpedo. I let my torso lean forward towards the water, tuck my head down, bend my left leg and push.

I lurch sideways and enter the water with a loud 'flop'. Never mind. I'm finally in and my arms are powering me to the surface, finding their rhythm. My first length's a bit awkward and the turn is jerky, but I'm managing to make my breathing more even. My leg is joining in instead of acting as an anchor. I concentrate on getting the double kick regular and straight, willing my arms to hold me in a line. I'm moving fast. Nothing's hurting. Ace!

Ten lengths, twenty lengths – my neck's feeling stiff. I must be arching the muscles, rising too high out of the water. I have to make my head relax so I can breathe more deeply. When I curl for my twenty-fifth length, I become aware of another swimmer in the lane next to me – a boy in blue Speedo trunks, who's keeping pace with me and turning when I turn.

Gradually, he starts to pull away. By twenty-seven lengths, he's about two metres ahead. By twenty-eight, he's lost me. We're not racing, but something inside me responds to his challenge. I want to catch up. I will my arms into a faster motion, but they are tiring.

At thirty lengths, I reach for the edge of the pool and take my goggles off, looking for my adversary. He's already out of the pool with a towel on, listening to a man in a tracksuit, who is correcting his front crawl hand posture.

How many times has Dan done the same thing for me?

The boy looks about fourteen and is very strong. He has a swimmer's physique – broad shoulders and six-pack stomach, still tanned from the summer. Muscles like tennis balls in his arms and long legs that are starting to sprout dark hairs. He has a few on his chest too, as if a spider had left its legs behind.

He takes his hat off and thick, black hair envelops his face and ears. He leans forward and shakes his head from side to side to clear any remaining water. He sees me looking at him and gives me a really great smile. I feel my ears flush hot with embarrassment.

The man pats him on the back and the boy starts to move towards the changing rooms. He really is in fantastic shape. Don't stare at him, Amy. What are you like?

'You gave Kel a run for his money for a while there.' I look up and the guy is standing there, right in front of me. 'What's your name?'

'Amy Curtis,' I reply.

'Mike Tindall,' he says, offering me his hand. I shake it with my wet one. 'I'm Kel's coach. Would you like a lift out?'

He helps me out of the water with one strong motion. I sit on the edge of the pool, conscious of my appearance.

'Could you pass me my leg, please?' I ask. Mike lifts Arthur without embarrassment and gives him to me.

'You know, you can have special swimming legs made,' he says. 'They fill with water and give you greater stability. Expensive, but might be worth the investment, if you're serious, and it looks like you mean business.'

'Maybe.' I shrug. Actually, I'm really annoyed Ramoul hasn't said anything about this option. I strap Arthur on and stand up so that I can speak face to face.

'You've got a great stroke there, young lady. Do you train with a club?'

'No,' I tell him, wrapping myself in my towel. 'I've only just got back into the water after my accident.'

Mike raises his eyebrows. 'League swimmer?'

'County champion, front crawl.' I smile. 'In Nottingham.'

'Heard of a bloke called Dan Madden? He's working in those parts.'

'He was my coach.'

'Well, well, well. I was his coach, once upon a time. Small world, eh?'

'Are you a full-time coach now?' I ask.

'Professionally retired, but keeping my hand in at local level,' he says, and smiles. 'I worked with the Paralympic team in the eighties and early nineties.' He holds my gaze for a long moment. 'Kel's doing well. He's been with me a couple of months now. He's a good lad.'

Ramoul is loping towards us in his lime-green trunks, carrying a bag of weights over one shoulder. Mike takes this as his cue to move away.

'Anyway. Nice meeting you,' he says. 'Talented girl,' he adds, as he passes Ramoul on the poolside.

'Don't tell her that,' sighs my physio. 'I get enough attitude as it is…' And with that, he bends down and secures weights to my left leg and both my arms.

I feel agitated. I don't like the thought that Mike is viewing me as a possible Paralympic contender, just when I'm starting to imagine myself 'whole' again.

Thirty excruciating minutes later, I'm back in the changing room, nursing aching arms and thinking about Kel. When I emerge into the reception area, hair dripping down my back, he is buying crisps from the machine. I'm really hoping he wasn't watching my efforts of the last half-hour, which ended with me writhing around on the poolside with cramp in my left leg and Ramoul actually standing on my calf muscle.

Mike Tindall is booking lane time at the desk. Mum and I are waiting to say goodbye to Ramoul, who always takes forever changing.

'Amy. Let me introduce you to Kel,' offers Mike.

Kel retrieves his crisps from the hole at the bottom of the machine and stands up. He's wearing a black T-shirt over jeans and Nike trainers. Very cool.

'Meet a county freestyle champion from Nottingham,' says Mike to Kel.

'Amy Curtis – Kel Stevens.'

Kel says 'hi' and offers me a crisp. He's got a really deep, soft voice. I suddenly feel very self-conscious and wish I'd blow-dried my hair properly. I must look like a sewer rat.

'I don't like cheese and onion, thanks,' I say. Amy, you dumbarse. You sound like a health-freaky spoilt brat.

My mum holds out her hand to Mike and introduces herself.

'I hear you know Dan,' she says.

'How is the old rogue?' says Mike. 'Haven't seen him for, let me see – must be seven years. Has he still got that old MG?'

'The red one with chrome bumpers?' laughs Mum.

'It must be an antique by now – a bit like me,' says

Mike, smiling. 'Anyway. Expect we'll be seeing more of your young lady. She's got a lot of potential.'

'She wants to compete again,' says Mum. 'But it's early days. She needs a club first – and the chance to get her fitness levels up again.'

Mike scribbles a number on a piece of paper and gives it to me. 'Speak to Jenny Long. She's on the committee of the ASA and is the secretary of the Brighthelm Swimming Club, which is probably the best one in the area. I might be a little biased, as I'm the coach. Kel here is one of our top swimmers. Maybe he and Amy could have a chat sometime.'

Kel nods, but he's just being polite. Why would he want to talk to a stupid kid who has stringy hair and a crisp phobia?

Kel and Mike have already left when Ramoul eventually emerges. Mum and I exchange glances. He's wearing a green shirt and lemon-yellow chinos. And dark glasses, even though it's nearly night.

'Dressin' for impressin'.' He winks at us. 'Jamaican band at the Concorde bar and the hottest babe on the south coast is picking me up in...' he checks his watch, '...precisely one minute.'

At that moment, a shiny blue Mini with big silver headlamps pulls up outside the reception. The driver is a young woman with dark hair down to her tiny waist. She looks like a model out of *Vogue*.

'Keen. That's what I like.' He grins at us. 'Oh, and Amy, it was good tonight. Sydney and I are very proud of you.' He gives me a high-five and surprises Mum with a hug before disappearing through the automatic glass doors, his kit bag and the weights over his shoulder. We watch the Mini disappear from view and then walk to our car.

'That boy Kel,' says Mum, looking sideways at me. 'Quite fast, isn't he?'

'I've seen faster,' I say, a bit defensively.

'Quite good-looking too.' Mum is grinning.

God, am I so transparent? I stare up at the cosmic saucepan in the sky, secretly making a pact with myself. He won't get the better of me, this kid called Kel. From now on, he'll be my target. Whatever he achieves, I'll aim to better it. Whatever records he sets, I will try to beat them. Stubborn Taurean, eh, brain? But if I'm a bull, Kel Stevens has just become my red flag...

~

From: rabidralph@hotmail.com

To: amycurtis@ntlworld.com

Subject: Sad news

Lamey,

I have some terrible news to report. The health and safety executive at the hospital reported Ralph on the grounds of being a hazard to hygiene and at

3.30 pm today, he was humanely destroyed. I am going
to scatter his ashes in Gnome Man's Land — the
location where we three had our happiest moments.
In sadness,

Harry x

From: **amycurtis@ntlworld.com**

To: **rabidralph@hotmail.com**

Subject: **Condolences**

Dear Poppikins,

I was greatly shocked to hear of the sudden and
unexpected demise of Ralph the racoon hat. Please
accept my sincere condolences. I will remember
everything about him with great fondness (except,
perhaps, the smell).

Yours, in sympathy,

Amy x

35

'Don't blink or you'll smudge it,' says Caz, ten millimetres away from my face. She's using her black kohl liner under my eyes, above the eyelashes.

'Sorry.' I wince. She sighs and uses a tissue to remove the blurred line. Both my eyes are watering and I keep wanting to sneeze. I'm not allowed to look in the mirror yet. The transformation might be too much of a shock.

'I can't believe you go through this every day,' I say.

'Perfection costs.' She grins.

'You don't need it – you're pretty anyway,' I state. Caz stops what she's doing and looks at me, surprised.

'You're the clever one. I'm the pretty one. That's what Granny May said when we were little. And that's how it is. Make-up helps me feel good.' She shrugs. 'I'm not confident like you.'

'That's rubbish,' I counter. 'You're taking ten GCSEs.'

'But I've never been a champ,' she says. 'I've never won anything or set myself a goal and worked for it, body and soul. You're lucky.'

'Yeah, right,' I say, mystified.

'Whatever happens, you'll always be Amy. And that's special,' replies my sister, stroking my lashes with black mascara. 'It was in the tea leaves when you were born.'

'You know Granny May is off her rocker. She predicted Mum would marry a Hollywood film star, have five children and live in a mansion.'

Caz grins, but she's not entirely persuaded. 'There,' she says. 'You're done.'

I brace myself to glance in the mirror and feel my eyes widen. The face staring back belongs to someone older than me, a young woman with stunning dark eyes and high cheekbones. Her look is Mediterranean. Her smile frames small, even teeth, which are white against her olive skin. Her mouth is full and deep red, the colour of Morello cherries.

'You look like Granny Jane,' says Caz. Dad's mum died before we were both born. She was half Italian and had studied art in Venice. Dad keeps her photo in our gallery downstairs. It's a picture of her in a white dress on a gondola the day she got engaged to our Granddad Hugh. I can see the resemblance, even though her hair is black and mine is brown.

'Thanks, Caz. It's great,' I say. 'You're really good at this stuff.'

Caz just shrugs but I can tell she's dead chuffed that I think she's artistic. 'There's a special effects degree course I've been looking at,' she says. 'I'm going to talk to Mum about it, see what she thinks. I could do stuff for films.'

'Maybe you're the one who's going to marry the Hollywood film star, have five children and live in a mansion,' I say. We both giggle.

There's a soft knock on the door. 'Taxi for Miss Curtis,'

calls a familiar voice, pretending to be the butler.

'Ready,' I reply and open the door. Dad nearly does a double-take. His face is a picture. Caz has trimmed my hair and plaited the sides. I've borrowed her jeans and black jacket and I'm wearing my trainers and a pink jumper. I look at Dad expectantly.

'So, what do you think?' asks Caz. 'She's like Granny Jane, isn't she?'

'I'm not sure you need all that make-up on to go to the cinema,' says Dad, looking at his watch. 'What time did you say we had to be there?'

'Five-thirty,' I say, stunned.

'We'd better get going then.' And with that, he's gone. I turn to Caz and raise my shoulders in question. She gives me a hug.

'Wait, wait,' she says suddenly, reaching for her perfume and giving me a squirt on my neck.

'Oh, did you have to?' I cough, the fumes going up my nose.

'You look great. Really. Go and have a brilliant time.' She follows me down the stairs. Mum is waiting at the bottom. She beams when she sees me.

'Wow, just look at you,' she says, all emotional. 'Wait a minute, I'll take a picture.'

She disappears for a moment and returns with the digital camera. 'Stand with Caz, that's it, get closer.'

We put our arms round each other's shoulders and

pull stupid faces.

'Not like that – nicely,' sighs Mum, just like she used to when she was teaching us how to paint with a brush. We both laugh at the memory and there's a sudden flash as the moment is caught for posterity.

'Now. Have you got your money?' she asks.

'Yes.'

'And your phone?'

'Yes.'

'And some tissues in case it's sad.'

'YES!'

'Mum!' says Caz.

'Sorry, sorry. Have a lovely time. Call us if there's anything…'

'I will. But I'll be fine,' I say, giving her a kiss on the cheek.

'Bye, then.'

Caz is ushering Mum into the lounge so that she can't come outside to wave me off. Anyone would think I'm leaving home for the last time…

The phone is ringing. Caz lifts the receiver and pulls a face. 'It's the snotgoblin,' she says in a whisper. This is her name for Dollop.

I'm shaking my head and Caz is telling him that I'm not there but I'll call back tomorrow.

'Thanks,' I mouth silently, as I close the door behind me. I hope Gus is OK. I feel very bad suddenly that I haven't called him once. I've been a terrible pretend sister. *I'll make it up to him, Soph. Promise…*

Dad's got the engine running. He waits for me to put my belt on before pulling away. I wave out of the back window. Mum and Caz wave back. 'So what's the film you're seeing?' Dad asks at last.

'It's about a girl from a slum who becomes Miss America,' I say. 'It's a comedy.'

'Who's the director?'

'I don't know.' Oh, lighten up, Dad. It's just a movie with my mates.

It's the first time Dad and I have been alone since that night we came home from holiday. There's a kind of polite silence between us. He seems a bit distant, wrapped up in his own thoughts. He's not the same Dad who used to stand on my bed and sing into my hairbrush. Maybe it's just that I see him differently. I think the accident has changed the way we all look at things. Perhaps that's why Mum has started painting stormy landscapes instead of flowers…

We pull up outside the cinema and I see Georgia, Rachel and Ally waiting inside the foyer. They're waving at me like idiots.

'They're here, Dad. Thanks for the lift. See you later.' I lean over and give him a kiss on the cheek.

'Amy?' he says, suddenly. 'Have a great time, kiddo.'

'I will. Bye,' I say.

Dad is still waving when I go inside the cinema…

36

From: amycurtis@ntlworld.com

To: rabidralph@hotmail.com

Subject: Measuring up

Dear Poppikins,

How are you? Where are you?

Hot news! I've applied for an IPC (International
Paralympic Committee) Classification, which means
that I have to pass some tests in front of
assessors — usually a doctor or a physio and
a swimming coach, arranged through the Amateur
Swimming Association. I'll be able to compete in
regional and county competitions against able-bodied
swimmers, as long as my times are up to scratch.
Trouble is, I need to do more than just front
crawl. They want to see backstroke, butterfly and
every sort of start and turn. And I've had to sign
a form to say I'll let them measure my stump and my
good leg. Not looking forward to that bit…

From: rabidralph@hotmail.com

To: amycurtis@ntlworld.com

Subject: Dumbarse

~

'That's no butterfly. That is a sidewinder. Holy Horatio…' says Ramoul, shaking his head.

I've just swum twenty-five metres of my least favourite stroke and have almost tied myself in knots. My mind's in freefall…

'Or maybe an octopus who is very, very confused…'

'You try it with one leg,' I spit.

Ramoul clicks his fingers and points to my goggles. I take them off and hand them over, angrily. He puts both of his feet inside the elastic, tightens it so that it holds his ankles together and proceeds to do a perfect dive into the deep end. He swims fifty metres of butterfly to illustrate the point. He gives me a drum roll on the side of the pool to finish.

'What am I supposed to do? Clap?' I grouch as he emerges next to me and flips himself up onto the side of the pool.

'Just saying, it's possible, that's all. You want this classification bad, don't you?'

'Yup.'

'The assessors are not going to make allowances for you being a squid.'

'OK, OK. I'll do it again. Can I have my goggles back?'

'Magic word?'

'Or else?'

'That's two words.'

Ramoul can be so annoying. He flashes me his whiter-than-white smile and holds them just out of my reach.

'So whadjoo gonna do, Amy Curtis?'

I'm making feeble attempts to grab them, without success.

'Something that involves a lot of pain for you,' I warn.

'Ooh. Now there's a temper…'

I suddenly push myself out of the water, stretch my left arm to its fullest capacity and whip the goggles out of his hand.

'Yeah, that's right, you are going to *reach* with those arms and stop being so lazy.'

'You could have just said that instead of making me do dog tricks,' I growl. 'And you could have told me that I could have a special swimming leg…'

Ramoul widens his eyes at this outburst. 'Thing with you, Amy Octopus, is you think you want it sooo easy. But I know what goes on in that crazy brain and you would not be satisfied if you win because of an artificial aid. You've got a badass attitude with me today…'

As usual, Ramoul is right. My anger translates into the best length of butterfly I have probably ever swum. When I touch the end of the pool and look up, Mike Tindall is standing there, speaking to Ramoul. Kel's stretching just behind. They must be waiting for my training lane. Worst of all, Kel has seen everything. I feel my ears flush hot with humiliation.

Afterwards, in the café at the pool, Ramoul gives me my new exercise programme and diet sheet. I read it and gasp. 'Fifty pressups? Every day?'

'Oh yes.' He nods.

'And spinach?' (Triple yeuch.) ' I'm going to look like Popeye.'

'You are going to look like one mean athlete,' he says, earnestly. 'The kind that says – don't mess with me. It's what you want, right?'

I look through the glass window down into the pool, where Kel is practising front crawl. He has a very easy stroke – strong and assured. My eyes rest on his fit physique for a moment. 'Dead right,' I reply.

I shower carefully to remove the last traces of chlorine and then take twenty minutes drying my hair. All this deception is wearing me out. But there never seems a right time to tell Dad.

Let's look at the options. What's the worst that could happen? Well, brain. He might hate me and never speak to me again. Or he might disown me and say he doesn't have a second daughter, like in *Fiddler On The Roof*. Or he might leave home, saying he can't live in the same house any more, surrounded by LIES...

Mum's feeling the strain – all that secret towel washing. And she's sold one of her stormy landscapes to pay for the lane hire.

It's time to come clean. I'll do it tonight, when we get home, so Mum doesn't have to waffle on about our fictitious late-night shopping.

Mea culpa – I learned that today in Latin. It means, 'It's all my fault.' It might be a good way to start...

When we walk in the door, Mum rustling her Asda bags, hamming it up as usual, Dad is in the kitchen, frying onions and garlic. It smells fantastic. Mum and I exchange glances. We can't remember the last time he cooked.

'How does aubergine parmigiana sound?' calls Dad.

'Mmmm. Wonderful,' Mum replies, enthusiastically.

'And lemon soufflé to follow,' adds Caz, who is wearing an apron and whisking eggs with a blender.

'Have we come to the right house?' asks Mum, clearly delighted.

Maybe it's a sign. Dad's feeling mellow and after a couple of glasses of wine, he'll forgive my deception and give me one of his big bear hugs...

And maybe frogs will fly.

The phone rings and I lift the receiver.

''lo, Ame.' The voice is hushed and trembling.

'Dollop. What's wrong?'

'Didn't phone me back.'

That was a week ago. Guilt suddenly courses through my veins. I had completely forgotten him. Poor kid. And after everything I promised… I take the receiver upstairs into my bedroom as we're talking. I don't want Mum and Dad to know I've let him down so badly.

'I'm so sorry, Dollop. Is something wrong?'

'Don't know what to do, Ame.'

'Tell me what's happened,' I encourage him.

'It's Mum. Locked herself in her room and won't come out. I can hear her crying all the time.'

'Sometimes people need to be on their own, Dollop. She's probably just feeling sad.'

'Stopped crying now.' He sniffs.

'That's good, then.'

'No, not good. She's really quiet. She's not saying anything. She's just sitting on the bed. Can see through the keyhole.'

'When did all this happen, Dollop?'

'Started crying last Saturday. Locked the door yesterday. I'm hungry, Ame. So are the guinea pigs. All the money in the pot has gone now. Had to pay the milkman.'

My mind is racing. Dollop's been trying to cope on his own for six days, all because I didn't phone him back.

'I'm scared, Ame.' His voice sounds small and thin. He is gulping air in between his words.

Mea culpa. Thoughts are tumbling in chaos in my brain. There's really only one solution.

'I'm coming, Dollop,' I say. 'It's going to take me quite a long time, but I'll keep phoning you so we can talk, OK? Everything's going to be all right.'

'Yes, Ame. Can you bring some hay?'

All my limbs are trembling. I stand in the kitchen doorway and must look as white as a sheet because Mum puts her hand over her mouth. I have no idea what I'm going to say. Tears start falling down my cheeks faster than I can wipe them away.

This isn't the confession I had planned.

37

We're on the M25, heading through the Dartford Tunnel,
following signs to the North. I keep trying to phone Dollop,
but he isn't answering. It's half-past eight and it's raining.

'I was lost in a desert on a horse with no name...' sings
a croaky voice on the radio. 'In the desert, they can't
remember your name, 'cos there ain't no one for to give
you no name...'

What sort of grammar is that?

Dad's fingers are tapping along on the steering wheel.
He has this fixed look on his face, like it is his mission to
save mankind and he's late for his fight.

Mum wanted to call the police, but Dad spoke to
Dollop who reassured him that he did hear Shirley crying
a few hours ago. She just wasn't answering when he
banged on her door...

Apart from one loo stop, Dad stays in the fast lane all
the way to Nottingham. It's a quarter to eleven when we
finally pull up outside the flats. The rain has stopped.
There are big puddles full of moonlight on the
pavements. Dad helps me out of the car. I'm stiff as
a board after sitting rigidly for the whole journey. My
teeth are chattering. In the rush, I forgot my coat. Dad
takes off his fleece and slips it over my head. It smells of

onions and aubergines. My stomach cramps, complaining about its lack of dinner.

We climb the steps and Dad rings the bell. I bend down and look through the letterbox. The hallway is in darkness, but there is light coming from the kitchen. Dark shapes are running about on the floor. I can hear several types of squeaking.

'Dollop, it's Amy. Can you open the door?' I call through the flap.

'Too dark,' responds a scared voice from inside.

'Don't be frightened. My dad's here. Everything's going to be fine but you need to let us in,' I encourage.

'Light went BANG,' moans Gus.

'The bulb must have blown,' says my dad. 'I'll get the torch from the car.' He disappears down the steps. There's hardly a sound, apart from the distant jabbering of voices on a television nearby.

Dad returns with the torch and shines it through the letterbox.

'There, Dollop. Now you can see,' I call. 'Dollop?'

Moments later, I see a large shape like a giant turtle, looming slowly towards us, on hands and knees.

'Coming, Ame. Don't want to squash the babies.' He reaches the door and unbolts it, opening it a crack. 'Be careful. They might run out.'

Dad and I move inside and close the door behind us. The flat has a stale smell of oven chips and old hay. The torch identifies hundreds of small, dark pellets on the ground. I count at least seven different guinea pigs running around, their startled eyes gleaming red in the white beam.

'Jesus Christ,' says Dad, under his breath.

Gus is back in the kitchen, sitting under the table, which seems to have become his home, as it shelters his pillow and duvet and several of Sophie's teddy bears. On top of the table are several dirty plates and mugs and the remains of frozen pizzas that haven't been cooked.

Dad tells me to look after Gus and give him some of the milk and cake that Mum hastily put in a bag. He knocks on Shirley's door and tries the handle. 'Shirley. It's Dave Curtis. I've got Amy with me. We've come to see if you're OK. Can you hear me, Shirley?'

There's no sound. Dad turns to me. 'I'll have to break it down,' he says.

'Wait,' I say. 'Let me try.' I approach the door. I've just thought of something.

'Shirley? Do you remember that time Soph and I locked ourselves in the bathroom – that day we were making witches' potions out of washing-up liquid and dried leaves? Soph said we were under the power of a black spell and the magic key would unlock the door only when the potions were ready. You said you didn't care if we never came out, because you and Gus were going out to tea. And if we weren't there, Gus could eat our cakes.'

Silence. Dad gestures for me to carry on.

'We heard the front door shut, and Soph started crying and unlocked the door. You and Gus were waiting on the landing with your coats on. And we did go out for cakes and you told us that it's really important not to lock doors because it frightens people and it can be very dangerous. Do you remember, Shirley?'

No sound.

'Not listening,' says Gus, quietly, his eyes downcast.

I look at Dad, whose eyes tell me this situation is very serious. He motions for us to get away from the door. He's going to kick it down. Gus and I move into the kitchen and put our fingers in our ears. Dad boots the wooden panel just under the handle. There's a loud splitting noise, as the wood shatters and the lock is forced through the frame the other side. He turns the light on. We all stare into the room.

There is no one there.

'When did you say you last heard your mum?' Dad asks Dollop, breathing hard.

'Got home from school. Heard her crying again,' he replies.

'You've been getting yourself to school?' repeats Dad, shaking his head.

'Can have brekky if you get there early,' says Dollop, shrugging. 'Bacon sarnies and omelettes.' He is crying now. His eyes have closed up and disappeared behind his cheeks.

'It's OK, Dollop,' I try to reassure him. 'You're not in trouble.'

'You didn't hear your mum go out?' asks Dad, gently.

'Watching *The Simpsons* with sound loud so I couldn't hear her crying,' says Gus, his voice sounding as squeaky as the guinea pigs.

Dad quickly checks round the bedroom to see if there are any clues, but the purple-painted space is neat and tidy. Nothing is missing from the wardrobe or the chest of drawers. There is just a shape in the flowery duvet where Shirley must have been sitting a few hours ago. The fibres have long since given up their warmth.

'Check next door,' says Dad and my heart almost misses a beat. He's asking me to go into my friend's den – a place where we spent so much time messing about and making plans. It's a museum now, a place full of memories suspended in time.

I turn the handle and move inside. The curtains are closed. Light from the street lamps filters through and I can make out the shapes of Sophie's teddies on her bed and on her shelves. They stare as if in shock – their glass eyes wide and inanimate. Last year, I could have recited all their names. It was a game we used to play. 'Toby, Oscar, Lady Buttercup, Tanglefoot, Tilly, William…' Now their identities have faded in my mind and it's just a roll call of shadows.

The light suddenly goes on, making me jump. Dad has

appeared behind me. He puts his hands on my shoulders. He's holding me because I am trembling, faced with the sight of Sophie's polar-bear pyjamas on the floor and her duvet, rucked up and half off her bed – probably just as she left it, the day she went out and never came home. I close my eyes to shut out the vision.

'I'm going to call the police,' says Dad, quietly.

Dollop hears this and starts crying more loudly. 'Haven't been bad,' he wails.

'We need to find your mum, Gus. And the police can do that much quicker than we can,' explains Dad. I can hear him tapping numbers into his phone...

Help us, Soph...

In my mind, I can see Shirley, alone in a storm-swept terrain, rain-soaked and ranting, surrounded by dark shapes and tangled tendrils. In the sky above her head, there is an eagle, its terrible wings outstretched, its beak open in a silent cry.

'Dad, wait,' I blurt out. 'I know where she is.'

~

It's almost midnight when we arrive. Rain is still hurling itself against the windscreen. Dad cuts the engine but leaves the ignition on so that the wipers carry on flip-flopping across the glass. The wide beam of the headlights illuminates untidy rows of stone crosses beyond the flint wall and the massive silhouette of the church beyond.

'You two stay here,' says Dad, but Gus is already halfway out of the door in the back. He is disappearing into the cemetery like a ghoul, crouching low against the weather, his jacket pulled up round his ears.

I'm not far behind. Dad locks the car automatically and follows us into the deep labyrinth of graves and tombs. Our feet scrape impatiently on the sodden gravel. Water runs in rivulets from the saturated tops of statues. Their heads are bowed in grief. Even the angels are weeping. It feels like we've fallen into a computer game and this is the maze of death. Any minute now, some fiendish monster is going to leap out in front of us, its jaws defiant and our fate will be sealed. My heart is pounding. Everywhere I look, I imagine tombs creaking open, revealing skeletons with jaws locked in terror, spindly arms reach)ng towards me, beckoning me to the underworld...

Dad has brought the torch. Its beam has found Gus, who is running now. There's an urgent shriek and he is suddenly on the ground, writhing, holding his knee, jabbering and pointing skyward. Above him, the huge wings of a dark eagle stretch like a cloak. Its body arches towards him, its talons the size of an adult hand.

'Ame, Ame!' he is shouting, shielding his head with his arms now. 'Get it off!'

'It's made of stone,' says Dad, helping Dollop to his feet. Raindrops are cascading down the length of his nose. 'Can you walk?'

'Yup,' sniffs Gus, limping bravely.

Not far now...

We turn a corner by a thick, twisted hedge, our clothes clinging to our bodies, our breath rising and curling like serpents around the overhanging branches of trees. Gus raises his hand with a gasp and points. Five metres away, a feral cat slinks across the path, its eyes like silver moons, its curved back sleek and agile, ready for flight. We blink and it is gone – silently shrouded in night.

Dad shines the torch ahead and moves it slowly from side to side. It reveals headstones and carvings – images of heaven dreamt of by grieving relatives. Chubby faced cherubs, maidens playing harps, winged horses, all frozen in motion... And beyond them, in the far right corner, where I once leaned and said goodbye to my best friend, a lone figure is sitting, slightly twisted, head bent, one arm raised to its hidden face, like in a still-life portrait.

Shirley.

Thanks, Soph. I owe you...

Dad approaches and holds out his hand. Shirley looks up. It takes her a while to register that we're here. She gazes from Dad to me to Gus. Her mouth opens and at first, no sound comes out. Then there's a deep, anguished moan, like the north wind sweeping across the Pennines, gathering momentum, an inhuman lament that seems to be echoed in the cemetery by a chorus of ancient souls.

And Dad is holding Shirley, lifting her from the

ground, resting her head on his drenched shoulder, standing fast until the cry is spent.

～

'I'll put the kettle on,' says Dad, yawning.

We're back in Shirley and Gus's flat. Our wet clothes are hanging over a clothes horse in the kitchen. Shirley has lent Dad and me some things. He looks a bit weird in her red jogging bottoms, which only just cover his calf muscles, and the T-shirt with 'Women Rule, Men Drool' emblazoned across the front.

Dad and I have cleaned everything up while Shirley and Gus have had hot showers. He's replaced the old light bulb in the hall. And for now, we've put the guinea pigs in a big plastic box I found in Sophie's room, lined with some newspaper I've shredded. They're sleeping now, after a dinner of frozen carrots cooked in the microwave.

We're sitting at the kitchen table, the four of us. Gus has his head on his arm. It's one in the morning. We're eating grilled French sticks with cheese on, crisps, tomatoes and apples, which is all that was left on the shelves in the twenty-four-hour garage we stopped at.

'Better now?' asks Gus tentatively.

Shirley nods. 'Just couldn't make it go away. Every day it got worse, the guilt – that I didn't stop it happening, that if it hadn't been for me...' Shirley looks down, overwhelmed with sadness. 'The tablets from the doctor worked at first, but they made me all woozy. I don't remember much about the last few days. Or locking my door and going out…'

'It wasn't your fault, you know,' says Dad, stirring the tea bags in the pink teapot with the wonky handle, bought as a second by Sophie and Gus as a present for Shirley, the Christmas before last. His eyes are saying that guilt torments him too, day after day, night after night.

The official's glasses are falling in slow motion. Splintered fragments glisten on the surface of the pool… That's where it began, where the ripples started to spread…

'Everyone expects you to pick up the pieces of your life,' Shirley continues, 'but your head and your heart are locked in that moment, and all your eyes can see are two beautiful kids, our kids, wrapped together on the ground, covered in a blanket of blood.' She takes a sip of the tea Dad has put in front of her.

'You've faced up to it, Shirley. You didn't run away, thinking you could file it in a neat box and keep the lid on,' says Dad.

'I'd have done the same, in your shoes,' she tells him, putting her hand on his arm. 'Fresh start, new faces, new direction. Why not? It's different for Gus and me. We feel her here. Sophie's part of this place. It's like a lifeline, seeing her in that chair or jumping down the steps or coming out of the school gate… I need that, because it's really hard to remember, exactly remember, her voice.'

Shirley's face crumples for a moment. She covers it with her hand.

'You were right to be angry with me at court,' says Dad, without looking at her. 'You needed our support. And we weren't there for you. We were so obsessed with our own situation. The fact that one minute, our lives were perfect, and then, overnight, it changed. I realised I couldn't hold any of it together. It was like the thread had been pulled and the whole damn lot was unravelling. There were people interfering in our lives – medics, engineers, physios, telling us what was best for us and for Amy. I couldn't make it better. I threw myself into work, took on more than I could handle. Left Ellen to deal with the fall-out. She's so fantastic and strong and I…' Dad's face distorts into a mime-mask, a picture of despair. He shakes his head several times and wipes his eyes. There are no tears. I think he must be all cried out.

'Look at us, Amy,' says Shirley, managing a smile. 'A right pair of gargoyles, eh?'

'Mind the wind doesn't change,' I say, remembering.

'Maybe it has, love,' Shirley replies, reaching across the table and giving Dad and me a big hug.

Strange locomotive sounds are coming from Gus's nostrils. He is snoring.

38

We're heading south on the motorway. It's raining again. Articulated lorries bound for Europe are sending curtains of spray onto the windscreen. The wipers are beating double time, like a pair of frenzied metronomes. Thunder rumbles ominously overhead. Nature's orchestra is tuning up.

Dad moves into the fast lane to overtake. I count three of them in a row – metal monsters – each with double sets of giant wheels on each side. I close my eyes. My hands are sweating, gripping the edge of my seat. I don't want to see the massive axles underneath the bodies, or feel the vibration caused by the lorries' huge loads.

'Don't let life pass you by,' sings jazz diva Betty Blue on Dad's compilation CD. 'Give yourself the chance to fly…'

In other words, *carpe diem* – live for the day. That's something else I learned in Latin…

We're back in the slow lane and there's nothing up ahead. Strange how that happens on motorways. One minute, masses of vehicles, the next, empty space stretching to infinity. We drive for about twenty miles, alone in the darkness, like a shooting star crossing the universe.

Then, in the distance, far up ahead, there is something moving in the road, darting backwards and forwards. It's hard to make it out through the rain.

'Dad, look…'

But Dad has already seen it and is swerving to a stop in the emergency lane. He immediately puts his hazard-warning lights on. From this distance, we can see that there are two dark shapes in the fast lane. One is unmoving. The other, smaller one, is scampering around it, nervously.

'It's a fox,' says Dad. 'I'll have to move it. It could cause an accident otherwise. Stay there.'

As he gets out, I turn in my seat to check on the traffic. There are bright lights, like luminous pinpricks, moving steadily towards us.

'Hurry, Dad,' I shout. He runs across the carriageway and picks up the lifeless body. He's coaxing the cub to follow him but it's afraid, hanging back. Dad's hesitating. The lorries are approaching fast. He won't have enough time to make it to the emergency lane. He'll have to stay by the central reservation.

Oh God, not again…

The first lorry is sounding its metallic horn in warning. Five seconds later it storms by, followed by the other two monsters closely on its tail. Our car shakes as they pass. The noise makes my whole body shudder.

'DAD!' I scream. As the last lorry passes, lightning sheets across the sky and rain lashes down with even more ferocity than before. I scour the darkness and all I can see are two shining eyes and the white tip of a small, frightened fox cub, watching me through the gap in the central reservation. Moments later, it runs determinedly across the road and into the fields on my left. I see its short brush disappear behind a gorse hedge.

Dad isn't far behind. Drenched, he lays the dead adult fox on the grass. There's blood on his jumper and hands. He gets back into the car, dripping, looking like an extra from *Braveheart*.

'She was cold. Must have been dead some time,' he says.

'Do you think the baby will be all right?' I ask, quietly.

'It's got a chance, now it's away from the road,' he answers, trying to steady his voice. I can see Dad's hands are trembling. He rubs his face impatiently and starts the engine, but doesn't pull away yet.

'Thank you,' I say, my hand on his arm.

'I wish I could have done the same…' he can't finish the sentence. I squeeze his arm tight.

'I know,' I whisper.

'When Caz was born, two weeks late and with lots of drama of course, I was flying back from Dubai and she was already half a day old when I saw her – all pink in her Babygro, gift-wrapped in soft blankets. When you arrived, earlier than we expected, impatient to get on with life, I was the first person to hold you. Even before Mum. You were this new, amazing, vulnerable being, and I was supporting your life in my hands. I told you I would always be there for you. I wouldn't let anything bad happen to you. And the last few months I've let you down, time after time…' Dad's voice is almost a whisper.

'No, Dad. You haven't,' I reassure him. 'I'm very proud of you.'

'And I'm very proud of you,' he replies.

It has to be now, before this moment of closeness is lost, before I bottle out. They must be said, the words that could shatter this warm, cosy climate of unconditional love and change our relationship for ever.

Why is life so complicated? Why do we have such trouble being honest with each other? It seems the more you love someone, the harder it is. And yet, of all people in the world, surely those we are closest to are going to be the most tolerant and forgiving?

I'm hoping, now Dad is out of his man-cave, that he will understand…

'I don't want you to be angry—' I begin.

'I'm wet, knackered, filthy and cold, but I'm not angry, Amy. Thanks to you. And Shirley,' says Dad.

My breathing has gone weird, like my lungs have shrunk to the size of mouse organs. The world is still. We're warm and safe in our time capsule. My dad is proud of me. I wish this moment could last for eternity.

'Have you heard of *carpe diem*, Dad?' I ask.

'Is it a band or a strange religious sect?' he replies, fixing me intently with his gaze. He looks scared, like he doesn't know where this conversation is going.

'It means live for the day.'

'Yes, I know what it means.'

'It's what I've decided to do. I'm training again. I'm good, Dad. And I'm getting better.'

Dad is staring ahead now, unblinking, taking this in.

'I tried to tell you, that night by the pier. But you said we couldn't go back to our old life… Mum said it would be OK. We didn't want to keep it a secret…'

Silence. I've heard of people self-combusting, going up in flames, leaving nothing but their shoes behind.

'I think—' says Dad at last.

That I am the most deceitful person on earth? That he'll never trust Mum again and that our family life is finished?

'I've been a complete – dumbarse. Amy?'

'Yes, Dad?'

'Would a second chance be out of the question?'

And suddenly, he's holding me really tight and my face is pressed into his wet jumper and it smells of rain and fox fur and Dad all mixed together. It's a fierce hug, with all the extras, and it feels like home…

39

The Easter holidays have arrived hand-in-hand with warmer weather. The park is full of spring flowers, tended by a team of grumpy gardeners from the council. The daffodils, which started coming up too early in February, have given way to bright red and pink tulips and irises, creating a blanket of colour near the paths.

Dad and Mum are taking me to my first training session with the Brighthelm Swimming Club. It's my first time in the water since being awarded my IPC Classification. The Amateur Swimming Association has decided, after watching me perform tests on the bench and in the water, that I can race against able-bodied swimmers in my age group. Luckily for me, Mike Tindall was one of the panel of assessors and it helps that during my recent training sessions, I clocked up some fast times for my 100- and 200-metre freestyle distances.

Ramoul, as always, was right about the spinach…

I wonder if the younger kids will scream when they see Arthur. I take several deep breaths in the changing room before emerging from my safe cocoon, an odd-looking butterfly.

No worries. When I reach the poolside, the club members, ranging in age from eight to sixteen, are already warming up, pounding up and down, churning up the surface of the water like frenzied fish.

'Hello, Amy,' says Mike, who is wearing his coach's sweatshirt. 'Glad you could make it today. We're doing some time trials for the galas which are coming up.'

It sounds like an invitation. I unstrap Arthur and lean him against the wall before slipping my goggles down over my eyes. Mike helps me get to the edge of the pool and I dive into a free lane. It feels like coming home. A surge of adrenaline pumps through my entire body, making it responsive and fluid.

After the warm-up, Mike puts us into four teams. He's going to time our fifty-metre freestyle races to begin with. I'll be swimming against another girl and two boys. The girl, Phoebe, is about half my height and very wiry. The boys are older, probably under-fifteens at least. When I look at them closely, my heart does a kind of hiccup. One of them is Kel Stevens.

Before long, we're standing on the edge of the pool, arms raised, heads lowered, knees bent (or knee, in my case), waiting for Mike's whistle.

'It's not win or bust,' Mike advises me quietly. 'Just see how you go.'

But the red flag is flying. Taurus the bull is pawing at the ground impatiently, waiting for the opportunity to charge… I'm so busy glancing sideways at Kel, my leg is starting to wobble and I'm tilting over to the left. No amount of hopping can prevent the inevitable tumble onto my hip, which hits the tiles with a resounding 'thwack'. Prat, idiot, pants-brain Amy. Now you've pulled a muscle AND handed victory to the enemy on a plate.

In a flash, Kel is the first person at my side, helping me up. He takes my full weight on his arm and lifts me in one fluid movement.

'Thanks,' I mutter, my ears red-hot with embarrassment.

'No problem,' he smiles. 'Lean on me.'

That's exactly what Harry said in his card, all those weeks ago. Brain, get a grip! This gorgeous, fit guy is holding me. Why am I wishing he was my mad email pal?

'Maybe we could have a coffee sometime. Talk tactics,' Kel adds. And suddenly, the pain that has travelled to the base of my spine and made me dig my nails into the soft flesh of my palms to avoid screaming disappears.

Dad and Mike are now beside me, checking for damage. Dad is still holding the copy of *Yachting Monthly* he was showing Mum a few moments ago. He hands me my towel and helps me to a bench.

'You're lucky you didn't break something,' observes Mike.

But I'm not really paying attention to him. My brain is

doing acrobatics, screeching 'Kel thinks you're cool' in a high-pitched voice. And maybe, if Kel thinks so, Harry might agree?

Phoebe and the boys take up their positions again and when the whistle blows, she's the first into the water, arms flailing like a manic windmill.

Kel and the other boy, whose name is Shane, take longer to surface, but soon ease into their long strokes, overtaking Phoebe, who is totally disguised in a halo of spray.

Shane is the first to take his tumble-turn. Kel seems to reach the air with a new mission and is pulling away with incredible strength. Phoebe is at least four seconds behind now, sails losing their momentum.

'Go, Special K, go,' shouts a group of sprocky ten-year-old girls on my right.

Watching Kel shark through the water, I forget the anguish of blowing my first chance of a race. His strokes are so assured, so seamless. The whole performance is fantastic to watch.

Brain to Amy. Admit it. He's not your adversary. He was generous and supportive just now, and even though you need stabilisers and a good haircut, he probably FANCIES YOU!

'Go for it, Kel, GO!' I yell, louder than anyone else.

~

From: amycurtis@ntlworld.com
To: rabidralph@hotmail.com
Subject: Birthday

Happy Birthday Poppikins!
Did you get my card? Thought you'd like the racing
car — but don't get any ideas!
Are you going out for that pizza with your mates?
Love,
Lamey xx

From: rabidralph@hotmail.com
To: amycurtis@ntlworld.com
Subject: Walking on air

Hi Lamey,
Happy 14th Birthday. Did you get my helium
balloon? Hope it was still inflated. It was
a pig to get into the box. Went out with my
mates and ate half a pizza and some dough balls.
I've put on a whole stone! Mum let me have a beer
and told me not to get legless. Quite funny, for
her. She's got a new boyfriend called Jake who is
a bouncer and is missing a neck and some brain
cells. He's OK, though. He bought me two computer
games. I'm very shallow like that. Tell me about
your presents, especially the one from your

sprocky sister. Got my latest blood results — all
clear. How about that parachute jump, then???
Harry x

From: **amycurtis@ntlworld.com**
To: **rabidralph@hotmail.com**
Subject: **Your news**

Hey Harry,
Wahoooooooo!!!!! You are soooooooo fantastic!!!
Amy xxxxxxx

40

It's a red-letter day – not the sort of red letter that Mum and Dad get from the gas company. It's special for several reasons. One – because it's a year to the day since I won my county title for freestyle in Nottingham. Two – because it's the first time I'll be racing for my new club against other clubs from the region. And three – because I'm lucky enough to be still here, a year on from you- know-what.

Oh yes. And four, because we're going to have a big party at home to celebrate and everyone's coming, including Ramoul and his girlfriend, Sheena.

Mum sold some flower paintings in the Brighton Festival Open Houses exhibition and said we could hire a marquee for the garden. It's beautiful, with a ruched top, covered in twinkly lights. Barker's been sitting in it for ages, just staring at them with his head on one side. He thinks they are stars and is confused.

There's a banner behind a long table with 'Congratulations, Amy' sprayed on it in silver paint, which makes me feel really proud. Actually, the words look a bit blobby because Caz's hand shook when she was doing it. That's probably because she's in love again. Her new boyfriend is called Ryan and he is captain of rugby, which accounts for his square shoulders and lumpy nose.

There are silver helium balloons decorating each of the ten tables where people are going to sit to eat their food. Mum and Caz have been slaving for days to make big dishes of lasagne and veggie chilli and masses of banoffee pies. (I was allowed to choose the menu as it's in my honour!)

Dad's organised a disco to come and set up at about seven o'clock. I'm not allowed to choose the music, apparently, because I only like 'rude rap songs' these days. There's been a lot of whispering and I guess that they have one or two surprises in store for me, probably involving Ramoul bursting out of a cake or doing some limbo under a flaming pole or something.

My mind isn't really on the party, though. It's focused on the outcome of the next few minutes.

I'm just about to get into the pool with the rest of my team for the warm-up. Out of habit, I scan the spectators' gallery to see where Mum and Dad are sitting. They are halfway up on the right side near the finish point. Mum sees me and gives a little wave. Dad's scratching his ear and looking at his programme. His other arm is round Mum.

Ramoul is sitting next to them, wearing a bright-orange T-shirt and girlie braids in his hair. I must remember to have a word with his style guru. I glance from him to the tallish young guy next to him. He looks familiar – maybe it's one of Ramoul's old patients. He's always bumping into them and telling me yet another amazing story of recovery and courage.

Yeah, yeah, yawn, yawn... But this gorgeous guy, with his wavy brown hair and wide smile, seems to know me because he's WAVING AT ME. Suddenly, I recognise who this is. I hear a loud scream and realise that the sound is coming from my mouth.

Oh my God. Harry Higgins. Living legend.

I wave back with all my might, until Mike Tindall blows his whistle.

Poppikins is going to be at my party! It's the most fantabulistic present ever. Tingles are tearing up and down my spine. I'm thinking so hard about him that I forget to breathe properly and water goes up my nose and down my throat. Gross!

Concentrate, Amy. You're behaving like a total duh-brain.

There are eight teams including mine. We're all in our separate lanes in the pool. The noise of over a hundred arms and legs carving through the water is totally exhilarating. You can feel the pulse of other people's strokes through the current and absorb the electricity building.

Back on the team bench, I start to experience a raw,

gnawing sensation in my stomach. It's not like the butterflies that I've learned to accommodate at various times during the last twelve months. This pain is hot and fierce and it makes my arms and leg feel weak and shaky. When I breathe deeply, in through the nose and out through the mouth, it seems to subside. When I just watch the swimming and tense my chest, it returns with a vengeance.

For the first time in my competitive life, I'm in danger from something I can't touch or see.

Fear. The fear of failing. The fear of letting my team down. The fear of looking stupid or deformed in front of all these people. In front of Harry.

I've been here before. It's the same fear that lurked that lonely night in hospital, when I could have disappeared into darkness for good. It's not going to claim me now. I won't let it.

I scan the spectators' stand again. Caz has appeared next to Dad, with her boyfriend, Ryan. And beside them, Georgia, Ally, Rachel and Debs. And more familiar faces – Shirley (who now has pink hair!) and Gus. And lovely Dan. They've come all this way for me – to celebrate my special anniversary.

I'm going to be sick. There's a strange, watery sensation in my mouth and my tongue suddenly feels like sandpaper. The commotion around the pool echoes in my head and sounds like a thousand rooks cawing over a corpse. My temples throb. My eyes are blurred with the steam and the chlorine.

Focus, Amy...

Time to cash in my Christmas wish. 'Just get me through the next ten minutes without a catastrophe involving vomit and stretchers,' I plead. I make myself study the results board and see that we're holding our own against Waders from Evenbourne, the current East Sussex champions, but are only narrowly ahead of the Hurricanes, from Hartings Heath. Every placing will count. Why did I ever think I could handle this pressure?

All too soon, my race, the girls' under-fifteen 100-metres freestyle, is being called. Mike Tindall, who senses I am panicking, helps me to the starting board.

'Just aim for the line and—'

'Get there,' I interject, trying to make my voice sound more confident than I feel.

'Exactly,' he says and squeezes my hand.

Our names are announced over the intercom. When mine is read out, half the people in the stands get up on their feet and applaud. My team is cheering – I can hear Kel's voice. Even my competitors turn towards me and clap. I almost fall over backwards.

I don't think I can do this. Ramoul, where are you? I glance up into the gallery. He's not in his seat. My eyes are darting, trying to locate him. It shouldn't be difficult spotting that lurid orange... And he's there, on the steps, only a few feet away. And he's holding out his hands, palms turned upwards.

'Swimmers, take your marks,' says the authoritative voice.

I move to the front of the board, my left toes hugging the edge for all they are worth. My eyes don't leave Ramoul. Mirroring his movements, I touch my head, my lips, my heart and bring my hands into prayer position. We exchange a big smile. I can see he's still grinning at me as I take a deep breath and curl my body down, bringing my arms forward and my palms together. I tuck my head into position and close my eyes, analysing how I will come out of this dive and correct any sideways drift.

Breathe, Amy...

My heartbeat is so loud, I'm sure everyone else can hear it too. It's hammering in my ribcage and will probably burst out of my chest any moment, like in *Alien*, creating a horrible gorefest on the tiles.

Concentrate...

'Go for it,' calls a soft voice. I could swear it's Sophie's...

As the whistle sounds, I leap towards the warm, blue water of uncertainty, every nerve, every muscle, every fibre of my being, body and soul, propelling me forward. This incredible, fantastic, exhilarating, totally spangly thing I'm doing is no longer just my dream. I'm racing again and I never want it to end...

~

There's this kid I know who can do weird cartwheels, eat a whole tube of Pringles, get showered and dressed in fourteen minutes flat, play 'Lord of the Dance' on the piano with her left toes, do a hundred and fifty sit-ups without getting cramp and pedal her bike backwards, perching on the handlebars.

She loves rap bands, especially the Mother Beepers, and her favourite thing in the whole world (apart from her family and her physio, Ramoul) is a warm, blue underwater world, followed closely by her dog, Barker.

She thinks that being fourteen and one of the fastest freestyle swimmers in the county is cool and that girls who like tattoos and reality TV are OK. She's someone who looks in the mirror every day (to check the hair and make-up situation), and enjoys shopping for clothes that show off her fab, fit physique and make her feel great.

She knows best friends will always be there, somewhere, no matter what. And that her brilliant new school and swimming-team mates will make every moment magic.

She hopes each morning the sun will rise, that life will be rosy and that the people she loves will stay safe.

She lives for today, because you never know what's around the corner.

And she's stopped drinking strawberry smoothies, because her boyfriend Harry says they give you acne.

The kid is me. And if you're wondering about the Olympics, watch this space...

ACKNOWLEDGMENTS

My thanks to Maddy, whose underwater skills created the first ripple of an idea; Christopher Pilkington at Endemol TV, where Amy began her journey; the dedicated team at the Sussex Rehabilitation Centre, Brighton – especially senior staff nurse Frances Tarr and the young patients who told me their stories; the sports development unit at Loughborough University for information on competitive swimming; Rosemary Canter at PFD for saying yes; Christine Lo at Orchard Books for encouragement to explore open spaces and wide skies; Sammy, for that snowy day in Notting Hill; my lovely friends, who make me go out and Joe Scourfield, whose laughter led me to Harry, and whom I was lucky enough to know. My special thanks to Chris, who has never lost faith, and to Bruce, the best big brother in the world.

ABOUT THE AUTHOR

Jill Hucklesby started writing poems and stories – usually about worms – when she was five. After attending schools in Sussex, where reports regularly referred to her 'perplexing lack of aptitude for maths', she studied for an honours degree in English and drama and then worked in theatre, journalism and public relations for national charities and arts organisations. She has written for the stage and for children's television and was nominated for a comedy-writing award at the Television and Performing Arts Showcase at BAFTA. This is her first novel. She lives in East Sussex with her family and Zack, the unruly retriever.

OTHER ORCHARD BOOKS YOU MIGHT ENJOY